I0668591

Frank Merriwell's Schooldays

OR

A Tale of School Life at Fardale Academy

By BURT L. STANDISH

Author of the famous Merriwell stories.

Edited by Jack Rudman

FRANK MERRIWELL
INCORPORATED
212 Michael Drive, Syosset, NY 11791

Frank Merriwell's Schooldays

MERRIWELL SERIES No. 1
ISBN 0-8373-9001-X

by Burt L. Standish
Edited by Jack Rudman

Copyright © 2014 by
FRANK MERRIWELL INC.
212 Michael Drive
Syosset, NY 11791
800-632-8888 • Fax 516-921-8743
www.frankmerriwell.com

For authenticity, the language, including slang and
pejorative expressions and references, however
unacceptable and offensive today, are included as an
accurate depiction of conversation and thought of the
early 20th century. To sanitize such references to
conform to contemporary sensitivities, would
compromise the literary accuracy of the work.

This edition is printed from brand-new plates made from
newly set, clear, easy-to-read type.

FRANK MERRIWELL'S SCHOOL DAYS

CHAPTER

CHAPTER

CHAPTER I

FRANK MAKES A FOE

"Get out!"

Thump! A shrill howl of pain.

"Stop it! That's my dog!"

"Oh, is it? Then you ought to be kicked, too! Take that for your impudence!"

A blow from an open hand sent the boyish owner of the whimpering poodle staggering to the ground, while paper bags of popcorn flew from his basket and scattered their snowy contents around.

"That was a cowardly blow!"

The haughty, over-dressed lad who had knocked the little popcorn vendor down, after kicking the barefooted boy's dog, turned sharply as he heard these words, and found himself face to face with a youth of about his own age.

As they stood thus, eyeing each other steadily, the two boys presented a strong contrast. The one who had lately been so free with foot and hand had a dark, handsome, cruel face. He was dressed in a plaid suit of a very pronounced pattern, had patent leather shoes on his feet, and a crushed felt hat on his head, wore several rings on his fingers, and had a heavy gold double chain strung across his vest, while the pin in his red necktie was set with a diamond that might or might not be genuine.

The other lad was modestly dressed in a suit of brown, wore well-polished shoes and a stylish straw hat, but made no display of jewelry. His face was frank, open, and winning, but the merry light that usually dwelt in his brown eyes was now banished by a look of scorn, and the set of his jaw told that he could be firm and courageous.

This was Frank Merriwell, who had just stepped from the train at Fardale. Frank had noticed the other boy on the train, and wondered whether he, too, were on his way to Fardale, but the haughty, withdrawn demeanor of the stranger had prevented any attempt at acquaintanceship.

Now, however, Frank had no hesitation in thus addressing the fellow who had just struck the popcorn vendor.

"Who are you, and what right have you to meddle?" demanded the haughty youth.

"My name is Merriwell, and I have a right to interfere because you just struck someone who is smaller and weaker than yourself. I may be a little direct, but it's my way, and I can't help it; I always take the side of the underdog."

"Do you mean to call me a dog? Take care! My name is Bartley Hodge, and my father-----"

"Never mind your family history; I don't care if your father is the President of the United States. You kicked that dog from pure viciousness, and you struck the boy because he dared to say a word in defense of his own. If he had been your size you wouldn't have hit him quite so readily."

"What about you? You're more my size."

"You probably weigh fifteen pounds more than I do, but you can try and hit me if you think you can. If you try to, I'll give you the licking you deserve, or my name's not Frank Merriwell."

Bartley Hodge hesitated. He was angry, but there was something about the looks of the boy in brown that made him instinctively feel that

Merriwell would be a hard customer to handle.

"Bah!" he cried, snapping his fingers. "I wouldn't lower myself to fight with you."

He turned and walked away, while Frank helped the owner of the dog gather up his spilled corn.

"Gee, you're really brave!" exclaimed the urchin, regarding Frank with admiring eyes. "That fella looked like he could beat you, but he didn't bluff you a bit. I'll bet you can murder him!"

"Well, I don't know about that," laughed the boy in brown. "But I think I would have been able to make it rather interesting for him."

"Have you come here to attend the academy?"

"Yes."

"I guess that's what t'other fella's come for. He's gone to look after his baggage. There's the expressman down at the end of the platform. He will take you and your trunk to Snodd's for half a dollar."

"Who is Snodd?"

"Why, he lives down at the cove, and he always keeps a lot of the fellas who come to git into the academy until after they are examined and accepted."

Then to Snodd's I go, but I think I'll walk. How far is it?"

"A good mile."

"Just enough to stretch my legs after the long ride on the train. I'll get the expressman to take over my trunk, and I'll give you a quarter to show me the way to Snodd's."

"Sure!" cried the barefooted boy. "I'll be glad to be your guide."

Frank sought the expressman, and gave him the trunk check, together with a quarter to pay him for moving the trunk, paying no heed to Bartley Hodge, who was regarding him with an insolent sneer. Then he returned to the young popcorn vendor, who whistled to his poodle, and they started on their hike from the station to Snodd's.

The station was situated on the outskirts of the village of Fardale, a place of not more than one thousand inhabitants. Fardale nestled among the hills which here reached down to the very seacoast, and, in the yellowish-blue haze of a warm spring afternoon, it looked like a very pretty little place, indeed.

It had been Frank Merriwell's ambition to go to West Point, but Harton Merriwell's influence had not been powerful enough to induce the Congressman from their district to recommend Frank, there being at least a dozen other applicants. So, as the next best resort, the boy was sent to Fardale.

Fardale Military Academy was modeled as far as possible after the great school at West Point, and was in many respects a most successful imitation. The students at Fardale, however, were a little wilder and harder to manage than those who went to the Point, for the fathers of unruly and wayward sons often sent them to this private military academy to have them "toned down."

For all this, not everyone could get into Fardale Academy, as every applicant was forced to pass an examination, and not a few of those who came to Snodd's as candidates for admission failed from utter unworthiness, being usually advised to return home and attend another school for a year or more.

Frank Merriwell became happier as he tramped along the road with the boy and dog for companions. He seemed to forget his encounter with Bartley Hodge until there came the rumble of wheels, and, looking around, he saw the express-wagon coming, with Hodge seated next to the

4

driver.

"Here comes that other fella," said the bare-footed lad. "He sure don't walk any, he don't. He's going to the academy sure, and I bet you and him has trouble."

"It is possible we may," admitted Frank, very quietly. "I am always making enemies, and I have started in first-rate here."

Bartley Hodge's eyes glittered as he saw the two boys and the dog. Without warning, he leaned over and threw a rock with all his might at the little poodle. The force of the shot sent the unfortunate little dog rolling and howling into the ditch.

In an instant, the happy look had vanished from Frank Merriwell's face, and he started forward a step, as though to rush after the wagon and drag the vicious youngster out into the dust of the road.

"Now I know he is a coward and a bully!" muttered Frank.

The barefooted boy went down on his knees in the ditch and gathered up the poodle, caressing and patting the whining creature.

"Oh, if I was big enough, I'd beat up that fella!" he cried, his eyes filling with angry tears.

"Never mind," said Frank. "I'll do it for you."

"Will you, honest?"

"Well, I'll do my best."

"He's bigger than you are."

"I know it."

"I'd just like to see the scrap," said the urchin. "Can't you fix it so I'll be there? My name's Tad Jones, and I bring milk to Snodd's every morning."

"Well, Tad, I'll see what can be done for you. Hey! I suppose that is the academy?"

"Yes, that's it."

5

Below them lay a beautiful, sheltered cove, with wooded hills beyond. At the western extremity of the cove were the academy and surrounding buildings, the chapel, gymnasium, mess hall and riding hall.

Frank was most agreeably surprised, for, as Fardale Academy was a private school, he had not looked for anything so eye-catching and imposing.

He stood surveying the place for some minutes, questioning Tad Jones who was ready with answers for everything, and then, Snodd's having been pointed out to him, a big old-fashioned house on the nearer side of the cove, he gave the lad the promised quarter and started down the road alone.

Little did Frank Merriwell dream of the struggles, trials, defeats, disgraces, battles, and triumphs that lay before him, and little did he know of the new life he was about to lead at Fardale.

CHAPTER II

FUN AT SNODD'S

It was not far from sunset when Frank reached Snodd's; he found his trunk at the door, and Snodd himself was there to meet him.

Mr. Snodd was a lanky, farmerish-looking man, with an ill-trimmed wisp of a beard on his chin. His clothes showed he was in the habit of making an effort to keep "dressed up," but apparently did not know how. He squinted keenly at Frank as the lad came up and asked:

"Are you Mr. Snodd?"

"Wal, yas, I guess I be," replied Snodd, as if somewhat in doubt himself. "Be you the fella what owns this trunk?"

"Yes, sir."

"Goin' to the academy?"

"If I am admitted."

"Hmm! Wal, you didn't ride over from the station?"

"No; I preferred to walk."

"Yas; saved a quarter that way. Now I don't know's we'll be able to keep you here. Ain't but one room left an' you won't want to pay what I ask."

"How do you know?" asked Frank, in surprise. "What gave you that impression?"

"Wal, I kinda calculated so from what I've heard of ya. I never let nobody beat me down."

"How much do you ask for the room and board by the week?"

"Four dollars, and that is cheap as-------"

"I'll take it, and here is the money for one week in advance."

Mr. Snodd gasped, slowly taking the money Frank promptly handed over.

"I kinda guess there s some mistake somewhere," he said. "Fella that come ahead said you'd try to beat me---said you was so blamed mean you walked over, 'stead of payin' the expressman another quarter to fetch ya."

"So Mr. Hodge has begun already," said Frank, grimly. "He was right; I did walk over, instead of paying a quarter to be brought by the expressman, but I wanted to stretch my legs, and I gave Tad Jones a quarter to show me the way here."

"Eh! Is that so! Paid a quarter an' walked! Wal, I guess you ain't so darned mean as ya might be. An' you've paid a week in advance, which t'other fella ain't done. I guess you're all right, an' if you'll ketch hold, we'll have your trunk upstairs in two shakes."

They carried in the trunk, and Mr. Snodd put his end down to introduce a buxom smiling girl who appeared in the hall.

"This is my daughter Belinda; Belinda, this is a new academy fella. What'd you say your name was?"

Frank gave his name and acknowledged the introduction, after which the trunk was carried upstairs and deposited in a small, neat room, the one window of which looked out on the academy building.

"The bell will be rung for supper pretty quick," said Mr. Snodd. "Better git ready to come down."

Then Snodd left him, and he immediately proceeded to wash and make himself presentable.

While thus engaged he heard a familiar voice outside, and he knew Bart Hodge was close at hand.

Frank opened his door slightly and peered out.

Hodge had met Belinda at the head of the stairs, and, considering himself something of a wolf, he was straightway doing his best to "make time" with the girl.

From his position Frank could see them plainly, and he also saw that the doors of several other rooms were slightly ajar, and he could see more than one curious, boyish eye peering from within.

Hodge was being watched by Snodd's boarders.

"You have a charming place here," said Bart, in his most suave manner.

"Do you really think so?" smiled Belinda.

"Sure. But it's not half so charming as you are yourself. I was afraid it would be rather dull here, but now I am sure I shall find it pleasant and agreeable."

"Hodge knows all the lines, all right," thought Frank.

Belinda blushed and looked down. She had a pitcher of water in her hands, having been on her way to one of the rooms.

"We always try to make it pleasant for all our boarders," she said.

"But I trust you will try to make it exceptionally pleasant for me," insinuated Bart, drawing a bit closer. "A moonlight ramble along the shore would be charming---with you."

"You are rather bold."

"I can't help it. Belinda--what a sweet name-- how poetic! You have the brown eyes of a fawn. The sight of those tempting lips makes me burn with a desire to taste their dewy freshness. Belinda, give me a kiss! Give me just one, and I will---"

"Get out!"

Splash! The contents of the water pitcher struck

him full in the face just as he was attempting to take the coveted kiss. With a gurgle of astonishment, he sat down heavily on the floor, gasping and dazed, while Belinda flitted away, laughing merrily.

"Oh, Belinda!" shouted one of the eavesdroppers. "How could you be so cruel!"

And a roar of laughter came from half-a-dozen rooms.

Realizing that he had been seen and overheard, Hodge scrambled to his feet and bolted for his own room, dripping with water.

Laughing at his foe's discomfort, Frank finished getting ready for dinner and awaited the ringing of the supper bell.

The boys trooped down to the dining room, where Snodd introduced Frank all around, ending by presenting him to Mrs. Snodd, a large, jolly-looking woman.

Hodge did not show up until the lads were seated and had begun to eat, Belinda serving. When Hodge appeared, the delay was explained, for he had changed his clothes completely, and removed all traces of the ducking he had received at the hands of Belinda.

His face, however, was flushed for he could not fail to note the sly grins of the boys as they were introduced. Frank was very grave, bowing slightly to Hodge, although he received no more than a cutting stare in return.

Being something of a ventriloquist, Frank resolved to have some fun with his adversary, so he made one of the other lads, Winslow by name, seem to observe:

"It is a very wet day, Mr. Hodge."

This caused the others to grin still more broadly, while Hodge stiffly returned:

"I hadn't noticed it, Mr. Winslow."

"What are you speaking to me for?" demanded Winslow. "I didn't address you."

"Yes, you did," returned Bart, sharply.

"You are a--a--mistaken," said Winslow, who had a peppery temper.

Immediately Frank made another fellow by the name of Gray seem to inquire:

"Mr. Hodge, don't you think Belinda is a sweet name--very poetic?"

"I don't know as it's any of your business what I think!" snapped Bart.

"Who are you talking to?" asked Ned Gray, as Hodge glared at him.

"I am speaking to you, as you had the insolence to speak insultingly to me first."

"I didn't say a word to you!"

"You did!"

Ned Gray looked as if he longed to punch Bart in the nose but, at this moment, Frank made Barney Mulloy seem to observe:

"When do ya expect to take that ramble along th' shore in the moonlight, Mr. Hodge?"

"I'll take a ramble with you, you Irish chump!" cried Bart, now thoroughly enraged; "and I'll punch you in the nose, too!"

"You'll what?" cried Barney, promptly rising to his feet. "Is it meself you're addressin' your remarks to, ya louse? I'll break ya big face!"

"Boys! boys!" cried Mrs. Snodd, in amazement and alarm. "What's got into you? You are behaving in a most ungentlemanly manner."

"That's so, by gum!" agreed Snodd. "Never knowed no fellas to act like this at the table before since we've been taking applicants to board."

"Excuse me," said Barney, as he sat down, "but it started me blood to boil to hear that critter call me a chump when I never said a word to him in all me life."

11

"Never mind him," Frank made Belinda appear to say. "He's in love, you know, and------"

"I won't stay here to be insulted!" cried Bartley Hodge, as he angrily tore out of the room, slamming the door behind him, but failing to shut out the roar of laughter that burst from the boys.

CHAPTER III

A COWARDLY ASSAULT

"Of all the nuts I've ever seen, that one takes the cake!" declared Barney.

"He didn't seem to like it when you asked him if he didn't think Belinda a sweet name, Gray," cried Sam Winslow.

"But I didn't ask him anything of the kind," rather warmly asserted Ned Gray. "I never opened my mouth to him until he spoke to me."

"Oh, come now!" exclaimed several of the others. "We heard you."

"I tell you you're mistaken; but Winslow fired the first shot when he said it was a very wet day."

"But I never said it, you know," cried Winslow. "I heard somebody say so, but it wasn't me."

"If this keeps up, Barney will deny he said anything about taking a ramble along the shore in the moonlight," said Ross Kent.

"An' it's th' truth I'd be speakin' if I did say so. I never said a word to him."

The boys looked at each other, greatly mystified, failing to observe the merry twinkle in Frank's eyes. As for Frank, he was not going to give away the trick just then, as it might afford him some sport in the future. He felt that he had squared with Hodge for trying to prejudice Snodd against him; but there was another account to settle. He did not forget that he had promised Tad Jones that he would give Bart a thrashing.

"I don't think one of you spoke to Hodge at all," smiled Frank. "I'm sure I didn't hear any one of you say a word to him until he spoke to you."

Frank spoke the literal truth, but the others were inclined to regard it as a joke. In order to divert their thoughts and prevent a further discussion of the matter, Frank told a funny story that seemed applicable to the occasion, setting the whole table off in a roar of laughter, and causing Hodge to be forgotten for the time.

Being a born diplomat, Frank decided that this was a favorable time to make himself solid at Snodd's, which he proceeded to do by keeping up a string of funny stories and witty sayings that convulsed the boys and made them decide that he must be a good fellow.

When supper was over and they trooped from the dining room, Frank was surrounded and carried off to Ned Gray's and Toss Kent's room, where there was a little "bull session."

"Make yourself at home, Merriwell," invited Gray, offering the only chair in the room. "Kent and I take turns at this when we do not have company. When we have company, we sit on the floor and let our feet hang down. Be patient until I produce the cigarettes."

He plunged headlong into his trunk, and soon produced, cigarettes, which he passed around, observing:

"Life really isn't worth living, fellows; have a cigarette with me."

"I seldom smoke," Frank declared, "but I will join you now."

As he reached out his hand, he noticed that one of the cigarettes seemed of its own accord to slip into his fingers, and he instantly decided that it had been "forced" upon him by Gray, as a sleight-of-hand performer turns up a card.

14

Instantly Merriwell was suspicious, feeling sure that the boys had gathered to see some kind of trick played on him.

"Fire away," directed Ned Gray, placing some matches on the stand. "Smoke up, boys!"

He set the example by lighting his own cigarette.

Frank was not backward, but he took care not to draw too hard on his.

Suddenly a dog was heard whining at the door.

"Get out!" shouted Gray, flinging a slipper against the door and settling back comfortably on the bed.

The dog barked angrily.

"Somebody drive that creature away, please," said Frank. "Dogs make me very nervous."

Ned placed his cigarette on the edge of the stand and went to the door.

This was even better than Frank had expected.

It had been his intention to attract the attention of the boys to the door long enough for him to light another cigarette with his, and to fling the one just lighted out of the open window. Now he proceeded to exchange his for Gray's, and no one observed the swap.

"There isn't any dog here," said Ned, in disgust, as he closed the door and came back. The creature must be outdoors somewhere."

He picked up his cigarette and gave a long pull at it.

Bang!

The cigarette burst into flame, and, with an exclamation of astonishment and dismay, Ned flung it to the floor, where it lay and sizzled, while a long, green snake seemed to writhe and crawl out of it.

Frank rose to his feet slowly as he said, "I'm taking this as a warning for what cigarettes can lead to--delusions, hallucinations, weakness. Never again---no more cigarettes for me!"

15

At that, he flung his own cigarette out of the window.

"Well, I'll quit, too, if I ever make another bungle like this one," declared Ned, rubbing his eyes and flushing as he leard the laughter of the boys. "You're the first fellow to come here and escape this dose, Merriwell."

"Then I have a lot to be thankful for," said Frank, smiling as he saw the green snake crumble to ashes.

"Say, me buccos," said Barney, "are ya in fer a bit of boozin' tonight?"

"Boozin'? Where? Fess up."

"Ya don't have to be Irish to know it's a right fine lot of cider Snodd has locked in the cellar. Lads, I know the way to get at it."

"Cider!" gurgled Ross Kent. Then, taking a classic pose, "Ah, nectar for the gods!"

"A necktie fer the gods!" exclaimed Barney. "I never heard it called that before."

"How can we get at the stuff?" asked Sam Winslow.

Barney replied with authority, "By the rollway door. I know a way to open it."

"Then tonight we drink, boys! Good old-fashioned hard cider can never be beat! Are you with us, Merriwell?"

"Yeah," demanded Barney, "are ya with us or against us?"

"I really wish I could, but I can't," apologized Frank. "I'm going over to the academy tonight to see Lieutenant Gordan. Maybe I'll go another time."

In vain they urged him, but they soon discovered that Frank was not the type to be coaxed into doing something aginst his will.

Frank stayed to listen to their big plans for a while. He soon decided it was time to leave and started out for the academy and Lieutenant Gordan.

Arrangements having been made by letter, Frank found that he was expected and was soon ushered

16

in. Before long, he and Lieutenant Gordan were quietly sitting in the latter's office. It was then that Frank's preliminary examination began.

Scarcely an hour had passed when the lieutenant declared:

"I don't think you have anything to worry about, Merriwell. If you just brush up on a few things, you'll coast through the exam."

After counseling Frank with his program, he walked him to the edge of the academy's grounds and wished him good luck.

Frank's spirits were soaring as he started his walk back to Snodd's. He had finally reached Fardale and it looked as though he would surely be admitted.

Of course, he had made an enemy of Bart Hodge, but he was not afraid of him. He felt that he could handle any situation that might arise.

Little did Frank know about Hodge's true nature-- vindictive and vengeful. Nor could he foresee the surprise that lay in store for him.

Frank was whistling a lively tune as he walked quickly toward Snodd's.

Suddenly, without warning, the bushes behind him parted and from out of the shadows came a stealthy figure who quickly surprised Frank, giving him a blow on the head that sent him reeling to the ground.

Before he could get back on his feet, his mysterious assailant was on top of him, pressing a handkerchief over his face while forcing him to the ground.

The handkerchief gave out a strong, pungent odor that seemed piercing to Frank's brain, and robbed him of what little strengh the blow had left him.

With his resistance growing feeble, he felt his senses lapsing into cloudiness.

All his efforts to cry out were ineffectual for he could emit nothing louder than a whisper.

Bright lights broke like rockets before his eyes,

17

and he heard the sweet music mingled with the tolling of the heavy bells.

Then these sounds drifted away--away--away--

CHAPTER IV

BARTLEY HODGE'S LITTLE GAME

Bart Hodge came to Mr. John Snodd's room as he was preparing for bed and whispered surreptitiously:

"Mr. Snodd, there have been burglars in your cellar tonight."

Snodd's lower jaw dropped in astonishment.

"Burglars! Are ya sure?" he managed to exclaim.

"Shh!" hissed Bart. "Of course, I'm sure. I saw them use the sliding door. I'm not sure how many of them were there, but I clearly did see them carry something away."

"Well I'll investigate this right off. I'll----"

"You'll only lose time if you do that. You may never find them," said Bart. "I know where they are; I followed one of them."

"Ya did, eh? Then, by golly, let's get at 'em! Just wait until I find my old gun."

In a few seconds Snodd was ready with his old-fashioned musket. Hodge advised him to take a lantern, which might be needed, and then they started out, taking the road toward the cove.

Bart was far in front of old Snodd, urging him on. However, he had not been able to communicate his confidence and assurance to the cautious old man as to what they were to find.

"I don't care about runnin' up against a gang of burglars," said Mr. Snodd.

"There's no danger of that," Bart confidently

18

stated. "Only one of them came this way."

Down near the shore, Hodge suddenly paused and pointed to a dark figure lying on the ground at one side of the road.

"What's that?" Snodd whispered, his teeth chattering with fright. "It's one of them burglars!" he said, excitedly. "If the critter jumps at us, I'll fix 'em!"

"Don't shoot!" cried Bart, catching the arm of the excited man. "I don't think he'll hurt us. He seems quiet enough."

Bart then advanced boldly, still maintaining an air of caution as he approached the prostrate form.

"What's wrong? Who are you? Get up, you!" hammered away Bart as he kicked the motionless body with the toe of his shoe. "Shine the lantern over here, Mr. Snodd. Maybe we'll be able to find something out."

Snodd's nervous apprehension caused him to fumble with the lantern in the dark. Finally, he was successful and gladly turned it over to Bart.

As he took Snodd's lantern, Bart said, "This guy smells like a brewery. He's probably smashed."

Snodd sniffed the air.

"By gum! You're right," he agreed. Mebbe he ain't one of the burglars after all."

Bart's plans were working like clockwork.

"Well, we'll soon find out. Roll him over and see who he is, Mr. Snodd. Do you know him?"

The direct light of the flame shining on the face of the figure brought gasps of astonishment, real or feigned, from the pair.

"What the . . .It's the last kid that came here to go to the academy!" exclaimed Snodd.

"You're right---it's Merriwell, all right. Has he been . ."

"Whew!" sniffed Snodd. "Can't ya smell it? It's cider as sure as you're born! There's one bottle, and another, and another----hey, they're my bottles! This is the stuff I put away six years ago. Here's a bottle that's got broke. He looks and smells like he's been swimmin' in it. He's drunk out of his head!"

"Oh, no!" retorted Hodge, as if he could not believe such a thing were possible. "He isn't drunk---he can't be!"

"I know when someone's stewed or not," fumed Snodd, his voice rising with his temper. "First he stole it and then he drank it all hisself."

Bart kept playing the role of the unbelieving, trusting friend while adding more fuel to the fire building up around the unsuspecting and unconscious boy.

"I can hardly believe he could do such a thing," he said as earnestly as he could.

"I wouldn't have thought it of him myself," acknowledged Snodd. "He seemed like such a respectable fella, but look at him now. He'll never get into the academy----they don't take no drunks!"

It took all of his self-control for Bart to refrain from laughing in his glee, but he managed to keep a straight face while in his heart he was crying:

"See how smart you look now, Frank Merriwell. Now I have you where I want you."

Snodd tried to wake Frank up, but to no avail.

"Wake up, young fella. C'mon, get up! I ain't gonna waste my time no more get up. You'll pay for this here cider and then you'll pack your duds and vamoose."

"He's out like a light," said Bart. "Let's leave him here to sleep it off."

"Well, I'll lock up the house, and then he'll have to pound around a while until I let him in. Stole my cider, did he! Wants to go to Fardale Academy, does he!"

"C'mon," said Bart. "Let's get out of here."

20

Snodd hesitated a moment, sensing vaguely that things were not the way they appeared. Again, he bent over Frank and sniffed the air.

"Seems ta me, there's something else I smell 'sides cider."

"I'm sure you're wrong," Bart said emphatically. "Let's go."

"Just pick up the rest of the bottles, boy. I ain't gonna leave him more juice to guzzle."

As they departed, they took the bottles with them, leaving Frank in his stupor. Bart had a hard time suppressing his satisfaction; in his mind, he pictured Frank being kicked out of Snodd's and being rejected by the academy, going back home in disgrace.

"His goose is cooked," thought Bart. "We're even now."

Mrs. Snodd and Belinda were anxiously awaiting the news of the burglars. When Snodd returned, he barely had stepped into the house before the questions began to fly.

"Did you find a burglar? Did you catch him? Did you fight with him?"

"We found one," answered Snodd, "but all he stole was my cider. He warn't in no condition to fight 'cause by the time we got there, he was loaded. We left him where he was---passed out as cold as a mackerel. Guess who it was?"

"Crazy Day?"

"Crazy . . . it's that new fella here---Merriwell---that's who it was. Ha, not Crazy Day."

Belinda and Mrs. Snodd were so surprised, a feather would have had no trouble bowling them over at that moment.

"Why, he was such a gentleman. I can't believe it," they cried in unison.

"If ya need proof, I sure got enough to suit ya: I saw him with my own eyes an' here's the cider that was layin' on the ground all around him. When he shows up after sleepin' it off, I'll kick him out personally and then report him to the academy."

It was sometime later that Frank finally regained consciousness. However, this was accompanied by nausea and a dull head throbbing as well as a full assortment of groans.

He slowly recalled what had happened to him-- the sudden ambush, the blow on the head, the struggle, and that strange odor . . . Was he robbed? No, had all his valuables: his wallet, his watch, ring . . . Why, then, had he been attacked? he wondered.

Not knowing how long he had lain there, he summoned all his strength to get back to his feet and started back to Snodd's. He was completely disheveled, his clothing was wet, and he reeked from cider. But, what was that other odor that still lingered--the same odor he remembered from last night?

When he arrived at Snodd's, it was dark and still; no lights were to be seen, and the doors were locked. He could knock on the door and try to wake Snodd up, but that would not be right. Instead, Frank wandered around the house, looking for some other means of entry. The curtains in Ned Gray's room were tightly closed, but the faintest glimmer of light could be observed filtering through them. Finding some pebbles on the road nearby, Frank gently tossed them against Ned's window. It did not take long for the curtains to part and for Ned's curious face to appear.

"Who's there?" he whispered cautiously.

"Frank --Frank Merriwell. I'm locked out. Could you open the door?"

"Sure, I'll be right down," responded Ned as he bounded for his bedroom door.

Frank stumbled over to the front door, feeling sicker than he had ever felt before in his life. The seconds he waited for the door to open seemed like hours. Finally, the door opened and Ned helped him in.

"Where ya been? It's after midnight."

"I went to the academy as I said I would."

"Oh sure, just the same way I took a trip to the moon and back tonight. Don't worry, I won't tell. C'mon to my room; we're playing cards and finishing up some of Snodd's booze. It's great. C'mon."

Frank could barely stand on his feet, and the lure of his soft bed and crisp sheets brought a quick refusal from his lips. Wasting only a few seconds to undress, Frank then dropped into bed and off to sleep simultaneously.

If he had known what awaited him in the morning, he would not have arisen so early. But, in complete innocence, he arose and dressed carefully, selecting a fresh suit in place of the cider-drenched one of the previous day. His head ached from the blow he had received from his mysterious assailant, and a lump glowed on that spot the size of a golf ball.

When the breakfast bell rang, he went downstairs.

Snodd met him in the hall, and said:

"The wagon's waitin' outside. Get your trunk and give it to the kid on the wagon. You can get your breakfast in the village."

Frank was astounded, "What? . . . Why? . . ." were the only words he could utter.

"I know you're a crook and a drunk, Frank Merriwell, and you're not a gonna stay in my place. Get out!"

CHAPTER V

HOW THE GAME FAILED

"Crook. A drunk. Mr. Snodd, are you out of your mind? What are you talking about?"

"You know what I'm sayin', boy. Ya know."

Frank's face became grim as he faced this verbal assault to his integrity without flinching.

"How dare you call me those names? I never did anything dishonest in my life, and I've never been drunk."

"Ya did pretty well on the cider last night, didn't ya? You were seen stealing it outa my cellar and acarryin' it away too. I seed ya with my own eyes passed out on the road, dead drunk, smelling to high heaven, with the empty bottles scattered all around ya. It's too late, boy. You're caught. Ya might as well give up and leave. I don't want riff raff like you in my place. Get your trunk---I'll help you lug it to the truck. I've got you dead to rights, kid."

Frank listened in wide-eyed amazement to Snodd's tirade. His first instinct was to defend his abused honor with his fists, but the seriousness of the charges against him brought him back quickly to his senses.

Quietly, he managed to say, "Mr. Snodd, you must have made some terrible mistake. I didn't do anything---I can prove it."

"I bet ya can," sneered Snodd. "If I saw somethin', I saw it. Don't ya call me a liar, you . . . you

24

. . .'Sides, I warn't the only one who seen ya---
Hodge was there.''

At that moment, Bart appeared at the top of the
stairs, his eyes gleaming brightly in triumph as
he stared at Frank.

"Too bad, Merriwell. I feel sorry for you now,"
he said mockingly. "If I knew it was you, of course,
I wouldn't have said a thing, but it was dark, you
know. When I saw four or five figures coming out
of the cellar, I naturally assumed it was burglars.
I told Mr. Snodd and we tracked down one of them
who turned out to be you. It really is too bad."

Frank began to fit the pieces together now.

"Mr. Snodd, it doesn't take long to see I've
been framed."

"Oh, sure ya were, kid," said Snodd hotly.
"The cider I smelt on ya breath was mouthwash,
I suppose."

"What time did you find me?" questioned Frank,
ignoring the sarcasm.

"'Bout nine-thirty."

"And what time did you see the burglars steal
the cider, Bart?"

"Exactly eight-thirty. I remember looking at my
watch. . ."

"That's too bad for you, Hodge. Lieutenant Gordan
can testify I was with him at the academy until
nine last night. My alibi is airtight. I couldn't
have been there with the burglars, Mr. Snodd."

For one second, Snodd seemed convinced; but
he quickly responded:

"If ya didn't do it, who did?"

"How should I know?"

"Ya know, all right. It's written all over your
face. C'mon, boy, tell me."

Frank stammered, "Well . . . I . . ."

"You just as well put the noose around your
neck, yourself---we know you let someone else

steal the cider and you got drunk on it. You're an accomplice and that's just as bad or mebbe worse 'cause ya didn't have guts enough to steal the stuff yourself and take the risk. Ya let someone else do your dirty work for ya. You're not the kind of a boy I want in my house---get out!''

By this time, all the boys were gathered in the dining room listening to the confrontation, as were Mrs. Snodd and Belinda. Suddenly, the front door opened, and Tad Jones, the little popcorn vendor, appeared.

''Is this the kid I'm supposed to take to the village for you, Mr. Snodd? He ain't no drunk. He's a good guy, I'll vouch for him.''

''Thanks, Tad,'' smiled Frank. ''I know who my friends are. I also haven't forgotten our little deal.''

Tad grinned.

''I suppose our deal will come off better than ever after this episode.''

''Mr. Snodd, I'm appealing to your sense of justice. At least hear my side.''

''I tell ya it won't do no good at all.''

''I want to tell you anyway. I was with Lieutenant Gordan until nine; he can tell you that. Then I started walking back here when, all of a sudden, I was mugged by someone who came from out of the bushes and knocked me out. You can see the lump on my head now--see? Anyway, I hadn't quite passed out when this fellow jumped on top of me and held something over my nose--a handkerchief, I think, and it smelled like chloroform or something like that. The next thing I knew, I was lying on the ground with a headache and nausea. At first, I thought I'd been robbed, but nothing was stolen and it isn't until now that I think I know what really happened.''

''That's all mighty hard to believe.''

''Don't you believe me? I've told the truth.''

26

"Nope, I don't. You'd better get."

The gleam of triumph was burning even more brightly now in Bart's eyes.

"Don't look so happy. Bart," muttered Frank.

"Me? I'm not happy. I really feel bad that I was involved in any way," he said hypocritically. "You could have made up a better story than that one, though. Nobody could possibly believe anything so fantastic."

"I believe it," declared Belinda, coming forward. "You can tell he's not lying by the look on his face."

Thanks, Miss Snodd." Frank gave her a grateful wink, "I'll always remember your trust."

Belinda was suddenly completely confused and blushed vividly.

"I have my proof," shouted Snodd. "Pack up an' leave!"

"Okay, I'll go," said Frank, beaten. "I see it's no use defending myself."

"Wait a second!" cried Barney Mulloy, forcing his way through the crowd of boys. "You're not gonna pack and leave 'cause efin ya do, begorra, we all will, too!"

"We sure will!" shouted the boys in unison, with the exception of Bart.

"Ya have to be a mighty low creature to do what you did, Mr. Hodge," continued Barney, giving Bart a dirty look. "Me fists are ready to pound you head in, you snake in the grass, you spy, you liar!"

"Mr. Snodd," began Ned Gray, "if you want to throw someone out for stealing your cider, you'd better kick all of us out. Cnly Merriwell and Hodge didn't have anything to do with it, we'll all swear to it. If you report one, you'll have to report us all, I want you to know."

It was now Snodd's turn to be taken by surprise. The thought of losing all his boarders horrified him.

27

"If all this is true," said Snodd, "how did Merriwell get all full of cider?"

"Oh, that was our little joke," said Sam Winslow, jolting everyone with surprise, and Bart Hodge, in particular. "Frank said drinking was against his principles. We thought that was a little corny so we ambushed him and used the ether. It was all a joke, wasn't it boys?"

"Yeah, that's just what happened," agreed the others. Only Hodge remained speechless.

"I guess you're innocent, Mr. Merriwell," apologized Snodd. "I think that was a mighty poor joke, but you shouldn't be punished for it. You others got to pay me for the cider, but I think everything will work out okay."

"Three cheers for Merriwell!" was the unanimous cry.

"Hurray, hurray, hip, hip, hurray!" roared the boys.

"Let's hear a boo for Hodge!" screamed little Tad.

A loud Bronx cheer filled the room. Bart's face was livid. He turned in rage and said:

"See if I care. If you had told me of the plan in the first place, it wouldn't have happened. I didn't know it was Merriwell."

Bart left the room hurriedly and ran upstairs to the sanctuary of his bedroom.

"Breakfast is ready," called Mrs. Snodd.

The roaring voices of the boys joined in for a round of "For He's a Jolly Good Fellow," as they marched into the dining room with Frank on their shoulders.

CHAPTER VI

THE FIGHT

"I'm really grateful to you for pulling me out of that mess," Frank said to the boys in Ned Gray's room after breakfast. "But, why did you do that to me for?"

"We didn't do anything," said Ned.

"But you admitted you did downstairs, not more than a half an hour ago."

"And because we did you're still here. We didn't know anything until Snodd said so."

Frank's face became clouded, "If you didn't, who did? I thought this thing was solved."

"Isn't it?"

"What do you mean?"

"If I were in your place," advised Barney, "I'd keep me eye on a gent named Hodge. If he ain't a snake, I'll eat me hat."

"I already have an old score to settle with him and now this . . . Mr. Hodge, watch out! Gray, I need your help as my second. Will you help?"

"Try and stop me!" cried Ned.

"All right. Good. Now for a little note to Hodge. Do you have some paper and a pen?"

"A fight!" shouted the boys with approval. "He's got to fight or he'll never be able to show his face again."

"Oh, he'll fight. I have no doubt about that. If he's assured a fair fight, nothing will stop him."

29

"Well, he'll have that, of course."

Frank rapidly wrote the challenge, put it in an envelope, and gave it to Ned who was to deliver it.

A little while later, Frank joined the others on the walk to the academy to begin studying for the entrance exam to be given in ten days.

In the distance, they saw a corps of cadets marching in precision formation across the campus and then into a large building. As he watched, Frank wondered whether all his present companions would pass the entrance exam.

Even though Lieutenant Gordan was so sure Frank would pass, Frank was not going to take any chances and began to study diligently: first brushing up on what he already thought he knew, and then going on ahead.

Bart was so sure he would do well, he refused to do any studying at all because it would be just a waste of time. He was openly contemptuous of all the red tape the exam involved anyway.

"This isn't the same as West Point," he said to one of the other applicants, who did not happen to live at Snodd's. "They won't turn down anyone here unless they have to, you can be sure."

"We have to start studying sometime, so why not now?"

"Baloney!" muttered Bart with contempt. "I'm not going to knock myself out studying in this place. Anyone who does, is a fool!"

Bart's unpopularity with the boys at Snodd's led him to make friends with the applicants staying in the village. Since he was loaded with cash and was a big spender, he did not have any trouble making temporary friendships.

When Ned gave Bart Frank's challenge, Bart showed no surprise. With a leer on his face, he tore up the note and sneered:

"You will be contacted by a friend of mine,

Gray, who will make the arrangements."

"That will be fine," said Ned stiffly.

Later that afternoon, Bart's friend, Hugh Bascomb, a moose of a boy from Michigan, showed up to see Ned. It was common knowledge that he had failed the examination at West Point.

Ned and Hugh resolved the plans. The fight was going to take place that evening in Chadwick's pasture, not far from Snodd's. Bare fists were to be the weapons and it was to be a fight to the finish.

Upon hearing the plans, Frank felt a little guilty. He did not like to fight but Hodge had changed all that. He owed him this fight.

Bart ate dinner in the village that evening and continued to make friends with the boys there. His success at making these casual connections was evidenced by his backing among the crowd later that evening when the boys gathered to watch the event.

At ten-thirty, the two opponents stood facing each other in Chadwick's pasture. Coats and vests were piled in a heap under a tree and their shirtsleeves were rolled up in anticipation.

There was little moon showing that night but the sky was nonetheless light. It was not difficult to distinguish one boy from another at a distance of several yards.

The news of the match had found its way to some of the cadets who had slipped away from the academy to also be on hand.

Bright flare-ups every now and then amid glowing circles in the night could be observed, attesting to the fact that the boys were smoking freely.

The quietness of the night prevented the boys from speaking in normal tones and only whispers could be heard.

Tad Jones was also there, nervous with excitement.

"Knock his block off!" he whispered to Frank. "Don't forget what he did to my dog."

Tad neglected to also mention the pain inflicted upon himself by Bart.

Frank had suspected all along that Bart was in some way responsible for what had happened to him the previous evening. The realization that Bart had done all he could to have him kicked out of the academy was enough to raise Frank's ire to a fever pitch and make him want to beat him unmercifully.

Ned gave Frank some last minute instructions before he stood up to face Bart:

"Remember, this isn't the same as a sudden fight, Frank. Usually I'd say, try to get him first and try to now if you can, but don't expose yourself. Keep on your feet and try to figure him out. In this way you'll be able to find his Achilles' heel, and then you can finish him off. Don't let him get you winded."

"Time!" called the referee, alerting the opponents.

The two enemies then stood face to face as their white shirts gleamed in the night.

"Shake hands!" was the stern order.

Both boys hesitated a little at first, but then Frank extended his hand which Bart barely touched.

"Fight!"

Both boys were on the defensive now: the fight had begun.

Bart made a quick rush at Frank who dodged it easily.

It was apparent that both young men knew something about the art of boxing. The spectators grew more interested. The excitement was building.

The dim light permitted their movements to be followed almost in silhouette: feint, cut, lunge, parry, dodge.

Then, suddenly, they were on each other.

The sound of one crack after another filled the air as fist and jaw connected.

Three blows followed in swift succession--- two light ones from Bart and a heavy punch executed by Frank which landed squarely on Bart's left cheek.

Bart stumbled, recovered, and jumped at Frank who safely dodged his advance.

The fight was fast and furious but Frank remained unscathed while Bart grew more and more angry.

"I'll murder you!" he bellowed as he let a round-house right fly at Frank.

"Was that what you were trying to do last night?" taunted Frank.

"This place isn't big enough for both of us, Merriwell!"

"Guess not!"

They went at each other furiously, but it could be seen that Bart was tiring while Frank was merely waiting for the right moment to finish him off.

Tad could not understand why Frank was holding back and he wished he could shout his friend on to victory.

Finally, Frank started his attack, and began to batter Bart fiercely. Soon he had Bart's nose bleeding profusely.

Two times Bart had tried to clinch to husband his waning strength but both times the referee intervened and forced Bart to resume fighting.

It did not take long for Bart to be sorry that he had ever started up for he received punishment at Frank's hands such as he had never received before. But he, too, had guts, he would not "chicken out." He knew how to accept his medicine.

No one, including Frank, belittled Bart's courage. He could only be admired for his tenacity in hanging on.

But Bart was becoming weaker and weaker with every blow until he could no longer put up an effective defense. Frank knocked him down time after time, but he kept bouncing back for more.

"Hasn't he had enough?" thought Frank, who could not bear to hit him any more.

All of a sudden, a great commotion ensued as a cadet jumped into the fighting area, whispering frantically:

"Everyone, get lost. Hurry up, Old Gunn's coming with Colonel Hicks. Get out of here!"

The pasture was cleared in a wink but Frank, feeling dazed and bewildered, found himself all alone.

He had to find his clothing before he could leave for it could be used as evidence against him if it were found by the Colonel.

Suddenly, he felt someone's strong hands on his shoulder.

CHAPTER VII

A PEACE OFFERING SCORNED

A frantic voice sounded in Frank's ear.

"Me boy, whatareya doin'? Do ya wanna get caught?"

It was Barney Mulloy.

"But my vest and jacket!" gasped Frank. "I can't leave them here. . ."

"Don't be a goon. The boys got your stuff all right. If ya get caught, then you'll never get into the school. C'mon. Here they come!"

Several figures could be seen running towards them rapidly.

Barney grabbed hold of Frank's sleeve and literally started dragging him away. As they started to run, they heard a voice call out to them:

"Stop where you are!"

"Oh, sure, we'll stop," muttered the Irish boy. "Mebbe we'll have a spot of tea! C'mon. They'll need wings if they want to catch us."

Recovering from his bewilderment, Frank had no trouble keeping up with Barney for he was a fast runner. Their pursuers soon gave up when they saw they could not keep pace with them.

As Frank and Barney jumped over the fence separating Snodd's land from Chadwick's they saw a figure who cried out:

"Is that you, Frank?"

"Yeah," answered Frank, a little out of breath.

35

"I just realized you weren't with us. I was afraid Old Gunn had gotten you," said Ned Gray.

"If it weren't for Barney, he would have. I owe you a lot, Barney."

"Ya can always count on me, me boy," assured Barney. "I'll stick to you as good as glue, I will."

"Hurry, let's get over to Snodd's. Old Gunn might be around here waiting," urged Ned.

Frank got back his clothes from Ned and proceeded to put them on as the three friends jogged their way towards the boarding house.

"One thing you can say for Hodge. He sure has guts," conceded Ned.

"He really does," readily agreed Frank. "I guess he can't be as bad as I thought."

"He wouldn't even holler uncle, he wouldn't."

"Probably not until he'd be unconscious. Everytime I hit him, I felt like a killer."

"Don't go feeling too bad, me boy. Methinks if the tables had been turned, he wouldn't of had as much conscience as you," said Barney.

"I agree," chimed in Ned. "He'd probably have put you through the wringer."

"Maybe, but. . ."

"No maybe's about it. He's mean, that's easy to see 'cause he's not ashamed of it. The only thing that kept him in there was his pride."

"We may all be wrong, Frank, me lad. But if I were you, I wouldn't turn me back on him for a second," warned Barney.

"I think everything is settled already," said Frank, who was never one to hold a grudge.

"Maybe he don't feel the same," responded Barney.

"That's not up to me. There's nothing I can do about it."

It was at that moment that Snodd's came into view. Everything looked serene and unruffled, but the boys proceeded toward the house with trepidation, hoping to find everyone there safe and intact.

The door was unlocked, so they slipped silently into the house.

"Who's there?" came a whisper out of the darkness of the hall.

"Frank, Barney, and Ned," replied Ned.

"Thank goodness!" exclaimed the lookout. "You were the last ones---we were all worried about you. Let me lock the door fast. Hodge is up in your room, Ned, with some of the others who are helping him with his cuts. Boy, is he a mess! Merriwell did a job on him!"

The four then walked quietly up the carpeted stairs to Ned's room. Ned knocked in a secret signal on the door and the key turned in the lock.

"C'mon in," Ned said to Frank.

Frank was not sure what to do at this moment. He figured that if he entered Hodge might think he was there to gloat over his victory, if it could be called that. At the same time, Frank also realized that this would be the best time to try to make peace with Bart.

Without any more hesitation, he followed the other three into the crowded, smoke-filled bedroom. The youths were discussing the night's events while they watched the first aid remedies being applied to Bart's bruised face.

Frank had no idea how embarrassing and uncomfortable this situation would be until he stepped into the room and was too late to do anything about it. Absolute silence greeted his entrance as the others just stared.

Finally, it was Sam Winslow who again tactfully took control of the situation.

"Hi, Frank," he cheerfully welcomed. "We were all wondering when you'd show up. Glad you came in, now we can congratulate you and Bart for your spunk and fair play. You were both great.''

''Yeah,'' agreed the other boys, ''you sure were.''

After hesitating again, Frank thanked the boys.

Bart remained silent, acknowledging the situation only by giving Frank a sneer.

It was a difficult and awkward situation so Frank decided it was time to break the ice with Bart. In a generous and modest way, he walked toward Bart and said:

''I'm really glad everything's over now and that the fight ended in a draw. Let's forget about it and let bygones be bygones. Shake hands with me.''

Frank then extended his hand to Bart with a friendly smile on his face.

Bart suddenly tore the wet bandages from his bruised face and threw them to the floor. He drew himself up stiffly and exclaimed in a voice choked with anguish:

''You know the fight didn't end in a draw! Just look at my face, then look at yours. You know you won tonight, but don't worry, I'll get even!''

''What's that supposed to mean?''

''That means I won't shake hands with you. Just wait until I meet you again---I'll fix you worse than you ever got me! You might have won the first round, Merriwell, but there'll be more! I'm not the type to forgive and forget.''

''Okay, have it your own way,'' said Frank quietly. ''I feel sorry for you.''

''If you had a little more decency, you wouldn't even be here now,'' Bart muttered bitterly. ''You know you won and you knew I was in here. . .''

''I came in to shake hands with you and call the matter quits.''

''And show everyone that you beat me. Well, you didn't!''

''I never said I did.''

"And you never will! Next time I'll be ready for you. I know all your tricks now. Just remember: this school isn't big enough for the two of us."

"Don't worry, I'll remember."

"I just wanted to make sure you did."

Then Bart sat down, replaced his bandages, and turned away, signifying that the interview was over.

CHAPTER VIII

"KIMBO"

All the boys agree that Frank had done the right thing and that Bart had showed himself to be a bad sport.

By his courage, Bart was raised up in the esteem of the boys at Snodd's and he might even have become popular if it were not for his bad showing after the fight. But Bart mistakenly felt that Frank would be considered the victor and he the vanquished so that any friendship between them would be impossible.

Bart later regretted the vow he had made to Frank about the both of them not being able to attend Fardale. He realized that if anything were to happen to his enemy, he would be the prime suspect.

These thoughts tormented Bart and deprived him of sleep. Twisting and tossing in bed that night, he was kept awake by dreams of deadly combat with his foe, awaking with clenched teeth and longing for the morning to come. Bart had suffered all that a proud and haughty spirit which has been drubbed can suffer and is certain to suffer. It was not until the dawn of the next morning that he was able to experience a few hours of the forgetfulness that comes from deep sleep.

Frank, too, had dreams that night, but dreams of another kind. His were of home, his girl friend, visions of success at Fardale Academy, and of happy days to come.

Bart did not appear at breakfast the next morning

and he also failed to show up at Fardale Academy that day, sending word that he was sick in bed. Since he was not as yet a student and his attendance was for his own benefit, no comments were made on his excuse and no one was questioned.

Fortunately for them, all the cadets who had attended the fight the previous evening had returned to their rooms undetected.

While on his way toward the Academy that morning, Frank was stopped by a Corporal Miles who invited Frank to his barracks while complimenting him on his fight. Frank had a strange feeling that he should not go, but Miles' ingratiating manner made the invitation so difficult to refuse, he went along with him.

They walked toward an unknown and mysterious section of the academy. Every now and then, Frank observed that Miles coughed strangely, which caused the three or four cadets on guard to stand rigidly with their faces turned away while they walked by.

As they approached a closed door at the end of a long corridor, Frank noticed that Miles was grinning broadly. Miles then opened the door for Frank and motioned for him to enter first.

Corporal Miles abruptly shut the door after Frank entered, leaving Frank to face alone about a dozen other cadets.

"Who are you? What do you mean by intruding in this manner?" queried a grim visaged cadet.

"Excuse me," stammered Frank apologetically. "I was invited here."

"Oh, really? By whom?"

"By Corporal Miles."

"By whom? There's no one in this academy by that name. No civilian has ever entered these grounds. How did you pass the guard?"

"Well, they turned their backs when I walked

by, and. . .''

"They what?" roared the hard faced boy, fiercely. "Do you mean to say that the cadets of Fardale
Academy were neglectful of their duty? Do you
dare make such a charge? Do you realize what
you're saying?"

Frank laughed nervously. "I'm not accusing
anyone of anything. I guess I've made a mistake.
I'll leave."

It did not take Frank long to discover that
it was not so easy to leave as it was to enter,
for the door had already been locked. It was
then that Frank realized he had been trapped
by the cadets so they could have some fun with
him.

"You're not going anywhere," said the apparent leader. "How do we know we can trust you?
You could be a spy aiming to undermine this institution or maybe even something worse. Who
are you?"

Realizing his predicament, the uncomfortable
civilian decided to play along.

"Frank Merriwell."

"Hmmm. . .Merriwell. Sounds familiar. Weren't
you mixed up in some kind of fight last night?"

"Yes, I guess so."

"Well then, will you tell us who your opponent
was and who else was there?"

Frank immediately realized that this question
might be a ruse which could be used against his
friends.

"No sir, I will not."

"What!" cried the cadet as if he could not believe his ears. "Do you know that you will immediately be condemned to suffer 'kimbo' if you dare
to defy me, Major General Hardtack, and the other
members of this grand general court-martial?"

"What's 'kimbo'?"

"it's a Greek word---the name of the worst, soul-racking military punishment."

"Well, I suppose I shall just have to suffer."

"This is your last chance. Do you still refuse to name those concerned in this disgraceful affair?"

"Yes."

"Even in the face of 'kimbo'?"

"Right."

"You're out of your mind!"

"Not yet, but I'll probably be crazy with anger when I get 'kimbo'."

"Major General Hardtack" signaled to the others to form a double circle around Frank. None of the cadets smiled; they all had the stern appearance of participation in a serious affair.

"Men of the grand general court-martial," began the "Major General," "what punishment do you recommend?"

In unison, they cried:

" 'Kimbo' !"

"Then his fate is cast. Bring the torture weapons."

One of the "tribunal" handed "Hardtack" a plug of very black chewing tobacco and a package of cigarettes.

"You will take a bite of tobacco, smoke these cigarettes, and sing a funny song all at the same time. This is just the first phase of 'kimbo'."

"But chewing tobacco makes me nauseous and I've never smoked more than a dozen cigarettes in my life," argued Frank.

"Too bad. I told you 'kimbo' was the worst punishment and there's more to come. You're going to regret you ever came to Fardale. Take a bite and chew! A cigarette is all lighted and ready for you. You'd better think of a song."

Frank's eyes were flashing with anger. He looked around the room, sizing up his opposition. He had

43

no recourse but to fight his way out.

The door was suddenly flung open and the excited face of "Corporal Miles" appeared.

"Scram, guys!" he ordered anxiously. "There's a pink haze on the luna!"

The room was cleared before Miles could finish his sentence. Only Frank was left, alone and dazed. The heavy sound of footsteps was heard and then Lieutenant Gordan's face appeared at the door.

CHAPTER IX

AN INTERRUPTED PICNIC

"What are you doing here, Merriwell?" demanded the lieutenant, his face grim with anger.

"I was stupid enough to accept an invitation to come here, sir," Frank honestly replied.

"Who invited you?"

"I don't know his name."

"Was it a cadet?"

"Yes, it was, sir."

"Then describe him to me."

Frank faltered again.

"I don't think I can. I didn't really look closely."

"Who else was in here?"

"Some other cadets."

"Could you identify them if you saw them again?"

"Even if I could, I wouldn't."

Lieutenant Gordan's face remained as stern and grave as before, but Frank seemed to detect a twinkle in his eye.

"The cadets have broken some very serious rules in bringing you, an applicant, into this unoccupied room. I wouldn't be surprised if they were up to no good. It's lucky for you, I felt something was wrong. I was just a little too late to catch them myself, but you can help me if you want to."

"No, I'm sorry, sir. I can't."

"All right," Lieutenant Gordan said with a faint touch of approval. "Now I won't be able to do anything but bawl out the sentries. You'd better not get yourself into a situation like this again. I'll make sure that you get out of here without any more trouble.

The lieutenant left the room with Frank following closely behind. The sentries saluted conscientiously as they passed, looking as innocent as lambs. They were alerted to the trouble in store for them when Lieutenant Gordan took their names down in his little book.

Frank was escorted from the building and beyond the border of the campus by the lieutenant as he gave Frank some helpful advice.

Frank realized how lucky he had been to escape safely from the pitfall he had let himself fall into. He shuddered as he thought of what would have happened to him if he had been forced to perform the first phase, and what would have followed that.

"Those guys are so anxious to have a hazing, they can't even wait until we're plebes," Frank muttered to himself. "Why'd they choose me, have I done something to one of them? Do they hate me already?"

Frank could not have known that he had been singled out because the cadets had taken a liking to him and wanted to test his courage. He also did not know that he had done the right thing in not identifying any of them to Lieutenant Gordan.

Frank decided not to say anything at Snodd's about this episode. The less said the better, thought Frank.

Everyone knew that a new plebe at Fardale Academy was ripe for hazing and, in this instance, the boys just could not wait. Having gained the limelight by beating Hodge, Frank had been picked to be "it."

Frank did not know what Lieutenant Gordan's investigation would conclude, but he hoped his captors would not suffer a heavy punishment since he bore them no grudge.

The next day, Belinda told Frank that she had invited several of her girl friends from the village school to spend Saturday afternoon picnicking with her at the cove. She had also invited Snodd's boarders to be on hand.

Frank accepted his invitation heartily.

Saturday brought about a dozen pretty, giggling girls. After all introductions had been made, the group marched off towards the cove with the boys carrying all the needed sports equipment and lunch baskets while the girls chattered on their way, leading the procession.

Among the girls, was one dark-haired, fair-skinned beauty to whom Frank was instantly attracted. She reminded Frank of the girl he had always dreamed about. It was as though he had known her all his life, but upon hearing her name, he realized that was impossible.

For a brief moment, Frank's eyes met Inza Burrage's, and he looked deeply into her large dark eyes. His heart skipped a beat and he felt a new sensation in his stomach. All his thoughts centered around this lovely as he forgot all about the girl back home.

Inza was a happy, light-hearted, unaffected girl, who seemed to pay no more attention to Frank than to anyone else.

Near the cove was a picnic area, complete with tables and benches, in a grove of trees. A few feet away, on a grassy field, was an archery target and a tennis court.

The girls set the tables and decorated them with wild flowers and ferns they had picked on their way.

The boys were showing off for the girls. Barney put on a performance any Irishman would be proud of, but had to be silenced by Sam Winslow lest the girls regard them as a pack of laughing hyenas.

Bart and Frank, although careful to avoid one another, were having a good time. However, it was soon obvious that they were both attracted to the same girl. It was then that it became impossible to separate them from each other's, and Inza's, company.

Bart, in repose, was an extremely good-looking boy, with a gentleman's manners and a beguiling smile, so it was not surprising that he was a great favorite with the girls. Frank found it hard to hide his annoyance that Inza seemed to enjoy his company.

When Bart became aware of Frank's attraction to Inza, he tried his hardest to win her attention. He swelled up with triumph as he saw his strategy was succeeding.

"I'll show him who's top man around here," thought Bart.

While some amused themselves by playing archery, others were playing tennis or were sitting and talking.

The tennis players drew straws to determine partners. By chance, the first four players were Frank, Bart, Inza and Belinda, but, to Frank's dismay, Inza became Bart's partner.

Frank, of course, would not show his disappointment and Bart was far too shrewd to gloat or to show more than the least sign of triumph.

Inza was a slight and graceful girl while Belinda was a little plump and, certainly, not so graceful as Inza. This made Frank even more upset since Bart's chances to win the match were greatly increased.

Inza began serving the first set. Belinda successfully returned her first serve, which was then masterfully volleyed back by Bart who put the ball away for a point without Frank's being able to touch it. Bart's triumphant chuckle at Frank's inability raised Frank's temper another ten degrees.

Frank was really a very capable tennis player and he realized that he had an equally capable opponent to contend with. Frank applied himself with determination and energy to the game at hand and, as the game progressed, he was able to demonstrate a high degree of skill and proficiency in the sport. But, Bart, too, was an expert. It was apparent that the match would be determined by the respective abilities of their partners. As Inza proved to be much more adroit than Belinda, Frank and his companion were losing consistently.

Frank could hear the girls whispering about Bart's great ability and he could barely contain his jealousy. He was tempted to invade his partner's area and return some of the more difficult shots that he was sure she would be unable to handle, but his conscience and sense of sportsmanship would not let him.

Halfway through the game came a startling interruption.

Running toward the crowd of young people was Tad Jones with his arms waving wildly, shouting something no one could understand at first. Not far behind Tad came a shaggy, four-legged creature running as fast as it could after him.

"What's he saying?" cried Frank. "Shhh, everyone!"

They all listened and heard him shriek:

"Help! Mad dog! Run for your lives!"

CHAPTER X

A TERRIBLE BATTLE

"Mad dog!"

Some of the boys took up the cry, and the girls screamed in fright.

It was a terrible moment of confusion and panic.

Tad was running for his life for behind him in hot pursuit was a foaming-mouthed dog. It was verily a mad dog.

"Run, girls! Get out of here!" shouted the boys.

Some of the girls were already making their way from the scene, but others were so fear-struck they remained frozen to the ground.

Inza started running into the woods, but tripped over a fallen branch and fell to the ground.

"My ankle...," she cried, "I think I've sprained it!"

Bart threw his racket to the ground and started to run for shelter.

"Help me, Bart!" called Inza out of her pain and fear. "I can't walk!"

Bart did not stop, but kept on running, ignoring the frightened, huddled girls as well as Inza's cries for help.

Belinda managed to plunge into the safety of the protecting woods.

Seeing Inza's plight, Frank quickly came to her assistance. Without the slightest hesitation, he deftly picked her up in his arms and carried her to where the other girls were huddled, gently placing her on the ground. He then turned around, drew a knife from his pocket and swiftly opened it.

"Frank, what are you doing?" cried Inza. "You're not going to fight the dog?"

"Yes, I have to!"

"He'll kill you! All he has to do is bite you and you'll die!"

"I know."

"Run, Frank! Get away from here!"

"And leave all you girls here alone to face it? It's better one should be bitten, not a dozen."

If ever a boy looked like a real hero, Frank Merriwell did at that moment.

Inza looked at him with a mixture of undiluted admiration and genuine fright.

Tad Jones was almost at the picnic area by this time, still shrieking his warning.

Frank now took several coats he found lying on the ground and wrapped them quickly around his left arm.

Tad dashed by and, in a moment, the dog was upon him.

Frank had never been in so dangerous a situation before. His face was drained of color, but he did not tremble or weaken. He placed himself directly in the animal's path while he watched the snarling, foaming, wild-eyed dog approach. Frank seemed to murmur something to himself before the dog attacked. It was a prayer for strength.

With a frenzied howl, the dog leaped straight for Frank's throat, its foaming lips snapping back to bare naked, gleaming white teeth.

Frank raised his covered left arm to break the force of the animal's assault. The dog's powerful jaws closed upon his arm, almost crushing it to the bone.

Although Frank had braced himself for the attack, the shock of the dog's assault was so great he had to summon all his strength to remain upright. Frank was able to reach over and drive the blade of the knife into the dog's left side, hoping to reach the animal's heart.

The force of the plunging knife made the dog release its hold on his victim, but it seemed to have goaded him on and made him even more ferocious than before.

Again the dog jumped at Frank's throat, and again it managed only to clutch the boy's muffled arm with its teeth.

All the girls were hysterical and screaming uncontrollably by now, horrified by the sight before them.

Only Inza remained silent. She had forgotten all the pain emanating from her sprained ankle. With her hands clasped tightly in her lap, she never took eyes from her protector.

"He's the bravest boy in the whole world!" she whispered through her pale lips. "Why should he martyr himself for us? How noble!"

Frank's face seemed to be made of stone. There was now a single expression almost rigidly etched upon it, one of intense determination to kill the mad dog and protect the girls.

Once, twice, the dog forced him to lose his balance. Once he fell to his knees and it seemed that the battle---and his life---were lost.

The coats around his arm were already in shreds. During the last attack, Frank thought he felt the dog's teeth go through his skin and crunch the bone.

Frank did not know how much more he could take for his strength was ebbing away steadily. Would he fail in his mission? Would the dog finish him off and then attack the defenseless girls? Where were the other boys? Why didn't they come to his aid with stones and clubs? Frank could only wonder.

It was almost over: he could not bear any more. A mist drifted before his eyes and he felt himself lapsing into darkness. A deep feeling of despair enveloped his whole being.

The fight was fast reaching a climax.

The dog again leaped for his throat. Frank had scarcely enough energy to raise his protected arm to fend off the renewed assault.

Once more he tried to stab the mad creature, but he felt the knife slip out of his hands.

He was now completely defenseless.

Summoning all the adrenalin he could into his system, Frank made one last effort. With all his waning strength, he seized the dog's neck in a headlock while the animal continued to try to bite off his arm.

Everything around Frank was becoming dim and hazy and he felt as if he were going to pass out. He could barely talk, but he tried to get out a warning:

"Girls, I can't do any more. . . Run!"

Something seemed to explode in his brain with a crash and Frank reeled to the ground, still grasping the dog's throat.

CHAPTER XI

IN A VAULT

The explosion Frank heard was the blast of a gun. Its muzzle had touched the side of the dog when it was fired.

Both boy and dog dropped unconscious to the ground.

"I got 'im! I got 'im!" cried John Snodd as he wiped his brow with his coat sleeve. "That critter ain't gonna bother no one no more!"

He had arrived at the scene during the last few minutes of the battle and he now explained his appearance to the crowd as he stood holding the smoking rifle:

"Tad came over ta tell us about this here dog. I sent him here to warn you all while I got ma gun. But while I was a gettin' it, that critter just ran by. I follered as fast as I could. I see I got here just in time, too."

"He's not dead, is he?" asked Inza.

"Sure, he is, by gum! I had the end of the gun agin him when I fired."

"I mean Frank. He was so brave. Now he'll die from rabies. It's just awful," she sobbed.

Mr. Snodd proceeded to kick the dead dog and then tried to wrest Frank's fingers from the dog's throat, which proved not an easy thing to do.

"Gosh, he sure got a death grip on the cuss."

The boys then took their cue and came scurrying

out of the grove, armed with clubs and rocks and appearing embarrassed and crestfallen.

Bart was the last one to appear and looked dully at Frank's body, asking in a genuinely concerned voice:

"Has he been killed?"

"If he hasn't been, it's not due to your efforts!" cried Inza. "You ran away and left him to face the dog alone!"

"I wanted to get a club," muttered Bart. "It was ridiculous to try to face it without a weapon."

"Sure. You didn't even think of anyone but yourself. If it weren't for Frank, we all would be dead. He's brave and strong and all the rest of you are. . ."

Barney was equipped with the appropriate words:

"A bunch of first-class cowards as I've ever meself seen, me included. I'll never be able to face anyone decent again."

Snodd bent down over Frank's limp form.

"I can't see no place where he's got bit. The stuff around his arm kept him protected, by gum!"

"He just fainted," said Ned. "Let's carry him back to the house."

"Someone go and get Dr. Brown from the academy," ordered Sam Winslow.

The boys either had to make a stretcher for Inza or carry her back to Snodd's. They decided on the latter course. Bart offered to carry her, but his offer was scorned in favor of Ned Gray and Ross Kent. All Inza would offer Bart was a look of complete contempt.

During the preparations for departure, Frank stirred, drew a deep breath, and opened his eyes.

Seeing Frank showing signs of life, Inza rushed over to reach him quickly, crying, "Water--someone bring me some spring water for him."

Inza quickly received the needed water, dipped

55

her handkerchief into it, and gently sponged off Frank's face while holding his head in her lap. Frank's eyes opened once more, and gazed directly into hers.

"You weren't hurt, were you?" he asked.

"You saved all of us. You were wonderful!"

"I did it for you," he whispered. Inza blushed.

Bart was carefully observing them. His hands and teeth were clenched tightly. His jealousy was thoroughly aroused.

"Merriwell's luck!" he sneered. "Anyone else could have done the same if they had thought of it."

Bart neglected to face the fact that thinking of the right thing to do and then carrying it out, were two separate things.

Bart then left the cove for the house, heartsick over the events of the day.

A little while later, from his bedroom window, Bart watched the group arrive. Ned and Ross were carrying Inza while Frank was following behind, surrounded by an admiring throng.

"He wasn't even scratched by that dog!" growled Bart, who no longer was concerned about Frank's welfare, but only felt an even more intense hatred.

Bart was right for Dr. Brown, after examining Frank, had come to the same conclusion. There was no danger of hydrophobia; Frank had completely escaped the teeth of the mad dog.

Frank had already recovered sufficiently to drive Inza home that evening.

The sight of them together brought Bart's jealousy into the open and he once more renewed his vow of vengeance on Frank.

Despite these vows, Bart made it a point to completely avoid Frank during the next four days. He remained aloof from the boys at Snodd's and spent most of his time in the village so he did not have to hear about how wonderful everyone thought Frank was.

The evening before the entrance examination, Frank was walking back from the village, having gotten his mail as well as a glimpse of Inza. As he passed the cemetery, halfway between the cove and the village, he saw a shadowy figure jump over the fence and disappear among the tombstones.

Frank wondered what a person could be doing in a cemetery at this hour, so he decided to follow him with great caution.

Near the center of the cemetery was a large stone family vault. In front of this vault, Frank saw another figure join the one already under surveillance. Frank was close enough to hear them talking, but too far to actually understand their words.

"I'll have to get closer," he said to himself with firm resolution.

Circling around behind them, he was able to get himself quite close to the suspicious, unwary characters.

He could easily hear them now and was plainly surprised when he recognized Bartley Hodge's voice.

"Bascomb, I'll pay you good money if you'll help me do this job."

"First pay up for having me show you this great place to put him in," said Hugh Bascomb, a village applicant for admission.

"All right---here it is," agreed Bart.

"Now, then, what do you want me to do? You have the key. Have you seen the place?"

"As I said before, I need help. I tried it once before, but it only ended up in a fight. I heard some of the guys at Snodd's planning to raid Snodd's cellar and I managed to steal some of the things they carried off. Then I waited for Merriwell behind some bush. When he came along, I knocked him out, chloroformed him, and doused him with some bottles of cider. Then I told Snodd I had seen burglars in his cellar and that I knew where one of them had gone. The old guy got a gun and followed me to where I had left Merriwell. Snodd thought he was drunk and was ready to give him the works if those jerks at his boarding house hadn't had everyone lie for him and promise to leave if he did.

"Snodd let him stay, but he still doesn't really know what happened to him. . ."

"I know now, Hodge," came a quiet voice from the shadows. "You just told me all I needed to know."

Bart drew back in astonishment from the approaching figure.

"Merriwell!"

"Yes, it's I and I have you to thank for explaining it all so clearly. Now I really know how rotten you are."

Hodge quickly recovered his composure.

"How'd you get here?"

"How do you think? I walked."

"You trailed me. You think you're such a great spy, don't you? Well, you're going to wish you never came here."

Before Frank realized what was happening, Bart had taken hold of him.

Crying to Bascomb, Bart said, "I'll make it fifty. . .help me now. . . Give it to him!"

Frank managed to rid himself of Bart's hold but was thrown to the ground by the force of Bascomb's blow.

"Hurry!" ordered Bart. "Open the door. Here, take the key!"

Bascomb's unwillingness was plainly shown

in moments of hesitation. Bart continued:

"I'll give you fifty bucks and our word's as good as his when we let him out. Which, of course, will be too late for him to take his exams. C'mon, hurry up!"

The rusty key was placed in the badly corroded lock. The bolt slid back and the heavy door was slowly pulled open.

Frank slowly came to his senses and realized what was taking place but could not tear himself lose from Bart's overpowering grip.

"C'mon, Hugh, give me a hand!"

Bart and Hugh dragged Frank along the ground and down the single step into the chilly, damp darkness of the vault. Once inside, they dropped him and ran out. Then Frank heard the lock clicking into the door.

He was a prisoner in a cemetery vault!

CHAPTER XII

ON HAND

Frank staggered to his feet and tried vainly to open the door, beating upon it with his bare hands and shouting for help.

The sound of his own voice echoed inside the stone room and scared Frank into silence.

When he began to think clearly again, he realized that Bart had won. Frank had up to now overestimated Bart's fundamental moral character and underestimated his perfidy and capacity for evil.

"He's going to keep me here until after the exam---probably until the day after. Who will accept my story? They'll think I was too afraid to take the test---that I wanted to get in without it. Hodge and Bascomb will deny everything I say. What can I do?"

Something in the vault moved. Chills moved up and down Frank's spine. His thoughts turned at once to corpses and ghosts.

Again, he heard something move and he pressed himself against the door in horror.

He heard a squeak, then another, and another.

Rats! He did not know how many or how brave they were, but these repulsive creatures brought new fear to his heart.

Trapped in a vault with rats!

* *

Examination day at Fardale was finally at hand, and the candidates made their way to the testing room.

Supervised by Professor Gunn, some cadets assigned the applicants to their desks and handed out the examination papers.

Lieutenant Gordan was present, looking in vain for Frank.

"Where's Merriwell?" thought the lieutenant to himself.

Finding one of Snodd's boarders, he asked: "Why isn't Merriwell here?"

Of all the boys, it just so happened that Bart was the one picked out to be so addressed.

"I haven't seen him for the last few days, sir. I wouldn't know where he was."

Barney Mulloy was close at hand, so Lieutenant Gordan continued his investigation.

"He wasn't in his room last night, sir, and not one of us has seen him today," said Barney.

"And none of you will," thought Bart triumphantly. "He's finished!"

Then Bart's mouth fell in amazement as the door opened and Frank entered with a cadet officer.

Frank was neatly dressed and appeared none the worse for his interment in a cemetery vault. Hodge turned pale and shook like a leaf while Bascomb was paralyzed with amazement.

How had Merriwell managed to escape in time?

Bart and Hugh now prepared themselves mentally for the expected accusation, but they were still unprepared for the next surprising development--- Frank completely ignored and avoided them as he made himself ready and settled down to take the test.

Bart found it hard to concentrate on his exam for he found himself trying to explain Merriwell's freedom and manner instead.

61

The test lasted two and a half hours. Some left the exam early while others required the full allotment of time.

Bart and Hugh finished a little before Frank, but remained outside the room waiting for him.

"Well, Frank," said Bart with a touch of bravado, "I see you weren't detained as long as I had planned. You have beaten my game. What are you planning to do now?"

"I'm not sure," Frank said quietly, "but you must have a pretty good idea of what I can do to you in this school if I so choose."

"You can't do a thing. You don't have a shred of evidence, only your word. For that matter, it's two of us, against one of you."

"There's where you're making a big mistake---you were seen as you dragged me into the vault. That same person released me and will testify for me if I want him to. Then you'll see how quickly you'll be admitted to the academy."

Bart and Hugh looked at each other, realizing that Frank now had the upper hand.

"Well, old boy," Bart started apologetically, "let's let bygones be bygones. What do you say? If you squeal and I'm kicked out, my Mother will be shocked. I admit I've been a lousy sport and I'm ashamed of it. Please try to forgive me."

"Me, too," said Bascomb with a great effort.

Frank generously complied since he was not maliciously vengeful.

"You both deserve the worst and I'd love to be the one to give it to you, but I won't squeal. At least, not now. You'd just better watch your step, though."

Bart and Hugh thanked Frank as he left them.

"We have to watch out for him," Bascomb warned.

"You're right," said Hodge. "He's dangerous and he knows too much for our confort, but what can we do?''

"Who can tell? But I'm going to bet there will be hot times in the future if we're all admitted."

"You can say that again!"

* * * * * * * * ***************

The next day, promptly at noon, the official admittance list of applicants was posted on the main bulletin board. An eager, uneasy group of interested applicants immediately surrounded the list, each one looking for his name. The names of Bascomb, Hodge, and Merriwell appeared on the list in their respective alphabetical places. Barney Mulloy, Ned Gray, Sam Winslow, and Ross Kent had also passed, although the names of some of their friends from Snodd's were not there, signifying that they had not been admitted.

Tad Jones was one of those on hand to congratulate Frank, but then he said:

"Why didn't ya do somethin' to those two guys? I knew old Bart was up to no good so I been follering him for two days. I hears him tell Bascomb to meet him at the vault, so I follered him there, too, even though I don't cotten much to graveyards. It was a good thing I went, boy, or else you'd never of showed. Eh?''

"You're certainly right. I owe you a big debt of gratitude. I couldn't expose them for what they did, the consequences would be too great for them. I don't mind a joke. This was serious, but maybe they've learned their lesson and will leave me alone from now on."

CHAPTER XIII

STILL ENEMIES

"Not me---I won't let them!"

"Yeah, you will, me boy. Just sit down."

"If you want to stay in Fardale, you'll have to, Hodge."

Frank Merriwell, in the process of dusting the mantle, was grinning broadly as he witnessed this conversation between Bart, Barney, and Ned. Frank nearly exploded into bursts of laughter as he watched a wrathful Bart pace furiously across the room and pound an imaginary assailant with his fists.

"What's so funny, Merriwell?" barked Bart.

"I'm sorry. I didn't realize I was laughing at anything," said Frank very quietly.

"You were and you know it!" snarled Bart with a toss of his curly black hair. "You looked like a hyena."

"Lookin' at a reflection of yerself," muttered Barney.

"What, Mulloy?" snapped Bart. "What smart comment did you have to make?"

"Didn't say a word to ya. Wouldn't waste me breath, I wouldn't."

"It's a plot! You're all against me!" accused Bart.

"You know that's not true," protested Ned. "We're not against you, but don't be ridiculous. Of course, we'll be hazed and made to do what-

64

ever the cadets want. You have to take your medicine like everyone else. Accept it.''

"My Father sent me here because the school bulletin said there wasn't any hazing here. I've been to other military schools, and . . . ''

"How come ya didn't stay? We wouldn't have missed ya!''

"What'd you say, Mulloy?''

"Not a thing.''

"Well, cut out that muttering when I'm talking. It bothers me.''

"Aw, it bothers ya, does it?'' mocked Barney, looking for trouble.

"Watch it!'' warned Ned. "We're going to have to cooperate if we're going to be getting trouble from the outside.''

"Four in a room. . .They have no right to pen us up this way,'' growled Bart. "My Father's very rich and he'll . . .''

"You can take it, Hodge. It won't be long,'' assured Ned.

"I'd be able to stand it if it weren't for . . .''

Bart's long gaze at Frank completed his sentence to everyone's knowledge.

Frank knew that even though Bart had said that he wanted to bury the hatchet, he was still not to be trusted.

Frank filled in the void left by Bart's unfinished sentence:

"Why don't you say it, Hodge? We all know what you mean.''

"Then there's no need to say it, is there?'' Bart sneered.

Frank put down the duster.

"I thought this whole thing was finished. You want to start up again?''

"You don't think we could ever be friends, do you?''

"I don't need or want your friendship, Hodge. I just want to know where we stand. Are we enemies?"

"I always like to settle an old score."

"And . . ."

"And I owe you something."

"Then we're still enemies?"

"It's finally out in the open, I'm no longer going to be hypocritical---yes! I hate you, Merriwell. I always have. I can't forget what you've done to me, and I'll never forgive you for it. I'm going to get even--you can be sure of it."

Frank's eyes and temper were blazing.

"And you've never done anything to me, I suppose. Don't you think I have a greater score to settle with you if you revive this feud?"

Bart snapped his fingers in contempt.

"That's what I think of your score. I can settle my own business. I haven't forgotten how you cheated me in the fight at Chadwick's . . ."

Frank exploded angrily.

"You call me a cheat! You know you're lying."

Bart clenched his fists and pushed forward violently.

"How dare you call me a liar!" he hissed.

"You heard me, you're lying."

Bart picked up a nearby chair and raised it over his head.

"Drop that chair, ye louse!" shouted Barney, trying vainly to stop Bart.

"On his head, I'll drop it!" answered Bart.

The chair flew through the air, struck a mirror, and crashed shatteringly to the floor with the smashed glass.

Frank had managed to avoid the flying chair.

Bart never had a chance to prolong the attack, for the sound of running feet was heard coming from the hallway.

In a flash, all four boys were standing at attention in the center of the room---heads up, heels together, eyes front, arms against their sides.

The door swung open and Cadet Corporal Burrage, his blue uniform fitting perfectly, collar, cuffs, and gold buttons gleaming brightly, and chevrons traced like pure gold on his sleeves. His face was set in the stern and grim manner of the officer. There was no doubt that he represented authority.

"What's all the noise I heard in here?" he demanded sharply. "Who broke the chair and the mirror?"

Silence. It was Bart's place to speak, but he remained quiet.

An angry light came into Corporal Burrage's eyes.

"Come on, gentlemen--talk! Who was near that mirror when it was broken?"

"I was, sir," said Frank.

"Why were you there?"

"I was dusting, sir."

"And by your clumsiness, you broke it. Report to Lieutenant Swift in room 40 right after supper, sir. You must learn that clumsiness is not to go unpunished."

Cadet Corporal Burrage slowly left the room leaving the four boys staring at each other silently Ned finally broke the silence.

"Why didn't you tell him the truth, Hodge? Why'd you let him put all the blame on Frank?"

"He had no right to put on so much rank, that dressed up baby!" answered Bart sharply. "I told you they'd never boss me around."

"Yeah, but look what you let happen to Frank."

"Well, why didn't he say something and . . ."

"Cause he has more honor in his little finger than you'll ever have in your whole body, you

67

dirty rat," cried Barney. "He'd never squeal and ya didn't neither have the decency to say something."

CHAPTER XIV

A MYSTERIOUS CAT

Frank reported to room 40 after dinner as ordered, and was sentenced by Cadet Lieutenant Swift to walk post in the hall until tattoo. Frank was not alone in this punishment as others were also present performing the same task.

Frank accepted his punishment gracefully and was soon pacing the halls, with his little fingers touching the seams of his trousers and his palms turned outward.

One of the other penitents was a chubby, jolly-looking Dutch boy who seemed to regard his punishment as a joke. Every time he and Frank met at their own posts, he always winked merrily at Frank.

"You just wait until I gets to be a lieutenant," he said guardedly to Frank. "You bet your life I vill make some other unsuspecting kid walk off the soles of his shoes to get even for this. That's the kind of a kid Hans Dunnerwust vas, and don't you forget it."

Frank had received strict orders not to say a word to anyone, so he was not about to reply to Hans' comment. At the same time, Frank realized how much fun he could have with him since he seemed to be so mischievous. Frank made up his mind to enjoy the situation.

A few minutes later, Bart and Hugh walked chummily down the hall together.

"Look at the captain of the guard, Bart, ole man." said Hugh grandiosely.

"Oh, don't bother me with such unimportant creatures," sneered Bart with contempt. The two boys strutted by slowly, waiting for Frank to show his anger so they could report him for breach of discipline.

Frank tried his best to contain his burning anger and kept silent.

"They'll be sorry," he thought to himself.

This incident drove all other thoughts out of Frank's mind until he saw Hans Dunnerwust come marching down the corridor with extravagant dignity.

Again, Frank summoned his ventriloquistic abilities and, making his voice seem to come from the other end of the corridor, he cried:

"Halt!"

Hans quickly came to a standstill.

"Right about face."

"At least, I know dat one," he said. "I vas alvays right about mein face."

"Carry arms," ordered the voice.

"Sure, I also carry a pair of arms---I'm not a freak, you know."

"Order arms!"

"Vat do ya mean? I don't vant some vooden arms vile I have two of mein own. I never ordered no arms, I bet my boots!"

"At ease, rest."

"Thanks, I vas getting a little tired."

Hans immediately sat down on the floor and leaned against the wall. He looked in vain to see who had given him the orders but could not see a thing.

"That's funny. Where'd that guy go? Maybe that vas part of the school discipline? Vell, I don't have to be told tvice to zit down."

Corporal Burrage unfortunately picked that moment to walk down the corridor for inspection.

Upon seeing Hans, he demanded angrily:

"Attention, sir! What do you mean by this?"

"Why are you sitting down while you're supposed to be walking post, sir?"

"I'll give you all the attention you vant. Go ahead," said the Dutch boy without rising.

"Get up!" ordered Corporal Burrage, now determined to use commands Hans could not misunderstand. "What do you mean by this?"

"Vell, I'm not sure. Maybe you could tell me vhy you're upset?" he said innocently.

"I made up my mind when I came here that I'd obey all orders if I broke my leg doing it."

"Obey orders? What orders? You were ordered to walk post until tattoo."

"Tattoo? I don't vant no tattoo on me, now."

"Why weren't you walking post as you were ordered to?"

"The other guy told me to be at rest."

"What other guy?"

"I didn't see him but he came by a little vile ago and gave me orders."

The picture was just beginning to be clear to Corporal Burrage.

"I'm afraid you're the victim of a practical joker. You'd better beware."

"Be vare?" asked Hans. "I'll be any vare you tell me to be."

"No---watch out for the pranksters. You'll get into trouble. Don't obey any orders unless you see the officer giving them. Understand? Go back to your duty. You are dismissed."

"Hey!"

Corporal Burrage wheeled around and turned back to Hans.

"What did you say? You never address a superior officer in that fashion, or anyone else in this institution for that matter. You always

70

use 'sir.' Can you understand that?''

"Ye . . . yes," stuttered Hans.

"Yes, sir. Say 'yes, sir.' ''

Hans obeyed the Corporal.

"Now, then. What do you want?''

"Vere is the post that you vant me to valk. I've looked everyvere for it."

"You'll find it. Keep looking."

Again, Corporal Burrage started to walk away, when a certain thought struck him. He listened closely.

"Meow, meow."

The noise was muffled, but was unmistakable. The Corporal could not detect from where it came but he realized mischief was in the air. If a cat were in the barracks, some joker had been up to his tricks. The animal must be removed.

Again the noise was heard.

Both Hans and the corporal looked around them.

"You heard it, didn't you?" asked Burrage.

"You bet your life, I did," assured Hans.

"Where do you think it came from?"

"I got no idea yet."

"Mee-oww!"

Burrage eyed Hans suspiciously since he detected the animal sound to come from somewhere in Hans' direction.

"You're not hiding a cat somewhere?"

"I don't usually."

Suddenly, a cat-like wail seemed to issue forth from beneath his vest. Hans clasped his hands over his stomach and turned a pale shade of green.

A look of astonishment, slowly turning to anger, was etched on the corporal's handsome face.

"How dare you, sir? Where's that cat?" cried Burrage.

Hans searched himself in vain for the cat.

71

"I-I don't know," he answered meekly.

An even louder shriek was heard. It was so loud and so intense, it served to scare the poor Dutch boy out of his mind. He quickly removed his hand from under his vest as if it had just been bitten by the cat.

"Guten Himmel!" exclaimed Hans, shaking with fear. "Vat's the matter with dat cat?"

"If you don't show me that cat right away, there'll be something wrong with you! You'll find yourself locked in the guardhouse if you're not careful."

"I really don't know vere it is, sir," Hans said honestly. "I'll give you five dollars if you find it."

"How dare you bring in a cat!"

"I didn't. You're making a mistake."

"You're making a serious one. You'll. . ."

A piercing shriek resounded.

Hans involuntarily stepped backward and lost his balance and fell to the floor. His fall was followed by a smothered howl that was appalling in its intense agony.

"Get up!" shouted Burrage. "You're crushing it!"

"I don't know how it got in my clothes," gasped Hans.

Another howl brought him to his feet.

"I wanted to change this suit anyvay, uh, sir! I'll be back as soon as I find the cat."

Hans ran straight away to the stairs, not seeing, in his confusion, that it was the wrong staircase to use to get to his room. Without heeding Burrage's order to halt, he reached the top of the stairs and accidentally collided with Professor Gunn who was on his way up. The professor was knocked off balance by the collision and fell down the stairs on his back with Hans seated securely on his stomach while clinging to the professor's hair with both hands.

CHAPTER XV

FURTHER TROUBLE

"Guten Himmel! I vas almost killed!"

The professor and Hans came to an abrupt stop at the bottom of the stairs.

"Help! Police! Murder!" howled Professor Gunn, thinking that he was being fiendishly attacked.

"Let go of me!" shouted Hans to the dazed professor, as he started to get up.

The two combatants rolled upon the floor.

"You're not going to get away!" gasped the professor. He then drew back his arm and landed a heavy blow on Hans' left eye.

The boy, not recognizing the professor, let his temper fly.

"You're not the only one who can fight!" he shouted as he took a punch at the professor. "I may not be a Jim Corbett, but I know how to take care of myself!"

In a flash, they were on each other, fighting furiously. The cadets, who had been attracted by the uproar, gathered around them to watch.

"Kill 'im, Old Gunn!" shouted one anonymous cadet, "show what you're made of!"

"Smash 'im, Dutchy!" cried another. "I'm putting my money on you!"

The battle would have continued indefinitely if some of the older cadets had not separated them and dragged the two apart. The belligerents then sat down and regarded each other, Hans covering his eye, the professor clasping his hands over his nose. They made a battered spectacle as they sat there in the midst of the roaring laughter of the encircling cadets, who could not contain themselves in spite of Fardale's strict discipline. Finally, realizing their danger, the cadets scattered, leaving a few to help the professor.

Professor Zenas Gunn then asked weakly, "What's all this about?" He glared at Hans. "Why did you assault me this way? Who's trying to assassinate me?"

"Vell, ya got me beat. I feel like I've been hit by a cyclone."

It was then that Corporal Burrage appeared with the needed explanations, to which the professor tried to listen with dignity although fully aware of his ludicrous appearance.

Frank had been shocked by the outcome of his joke and was afraid he had gotten Hans into serious trouble. He was hoping Hans would be shown leniency in view of the circumstances so that he might get off with slight, if any, punishment.

Not wanting to confess the truth because of the future value of his ventriloquistic abilities, Frank held back. If any real danger to Hans should have presented itself, Frank would have admitted the truth immediately. He would never permit another to suffer for his own misdeeds.

Frank remained pacing the corridor above as if nothing had occurred.

Below, the cadets were scattered, and Hans was marched away, led by Professor Gunn and surrounded by many cadets. Corporal Burrage was still unable to produce the cat so he presumed the animal had fled when Hans fell downstairs.

Frank had successfully broken the monotony

74

of walking post, so he resumed his task, pacing back and forth silently while listening to the distant strains of a marching band outside. This is the way he spent his entire evening.

When Frank returned to his room, he overheard a very heated discussion being conducted in his room by his roommates. He first heard Bart declaring loudly: "No one had better even try hazing me or they'll be sorry. I've taken enough at this school. I won't take another insult."

"What are you going to do?" asked Ned.

"I'll fight," Bart replied fiercely, and gave the appearance he meant everything he said.

"You'll be worse off, you know."

"If I ever find out who's doing the hazing, I'll report them so fast . . ."

"And you'll be marked for abuse as long as you stay here."

"I don't agree. You guys give in too easily. If you all showed some spirit, some defiance, the cadets wouldn't think you're such pushovers."

Frank remained silent as he approached Barney, already in the process of changing for bed.

"What's going on?" asked Frank.

"Who knows?" replied the Irish boy. "It seems that Bart's heard he's going to be put through the mill very soon."

"What happened to Hans?"

"Not a thing."

"They let him go?"

"They sure enough did."

"But he didn't come back to his post."

"Nope, they sent him straight to his room to have a steak put over his eye where Ole Gunn smashed him. Is it a mess! Begorra! Some of de boys met him outside after 'is eye was fixed-- did they have fun with 'im. You'd die laughing to hear him talk about the cat that crawled into his pants but he never knew where. Dutchy said it was a screamin' and a yellin' to beat the band, but he couldn't find it until he slipped and sat down. It let out such a howl, he figured it must have been in his hip pocket. He was so startled, he began to run for his room and ran into the professor instead. You'd bust your gut if you was to hear him describe how easy he slid down the stairs, seated on the professor's digestive track. By me soul, Dutchy is the funniest character I've ever come across in me life!"

Barney continued to laugh hysterically until he was purple in the face.

At the same time, Bart continued to rant and rave about hazing until Frank suddenly said: "Taps will blow in one minute, Mr. Hodge. I'm supposed to turn off the light promptly when taps are sounded."

Everyone but Bart was ready for bed. Bart hesitated and gave Frank a dirty look, but remained silent. He made no move to undress.

In a moment, taps sounded.

Frank walked quickly over to the lamp, but Bart intercepted him, saying:

"Don't bother; I'll do it."

"But that's my chore this week."

"Never mind, I'll do it tonight."

"I don't let other people do my duties for me."

Bart's lips curled in hatred.

"Aren't you noble! A perfect slave of duty! Before long, you'll be a big shot among all the cadets at Fardale. You'll probably be Old Gunn's special pet, too!"

Frank clenched his teeth in anger but held back his temper, saying quietly:

"Move away, Mr. Hodge. I have a job to do."

"Don't act like such a phony to me. I'll take

care of the lamp, so just get into bed."

With a quick step and strong sweep of his arm, Frank pushed Bart aside and took care of the light.

Bart struck back at Frank with a blow landing on Frank's neck, sending him staggering in the darkness. He recovered as quickly as he could, hearing a rush of feet and a savage panting by his side.

"Keep away, Hodge!" he warned.

"You're through now!" Bart hissed vindictively in his ear.

Then the foes clinched and a desperate struggle began in the darkness.

CHAPTER XVI

VISITED BY THE "JOLLY FIENDS"

"Cut it out!" warned Ned, trying to intercede between the fighting boys. "The whole school will be in here in a moment."

"Who cares?" snarled Bart. "I'm going to settle my account with Merriwell, here and now!"

Crash! Thud!

"Are ya all right, me bucco? Frankie, you okay?" came Barney's voice anxiously.

"I think I am," answered Frank slowly.

"What happened?" whispered Ned cautiously.

"I hit Bart. It was by accident, but I think I've knocked him out."

"Great!" exclaimed Barney. "Hurray!"

"I hope no one heard the fight," said Frank anxiously. "Shh! I hear someone coming! Get into bed, Gray! I'll put Hodge next to you. Hurry!"

Hurry, they did. Ned leaped quickly into bed as Frank lifted Bart off the floor, depositing him at Ned's side. They then rapidly covered the unconscious boy up to his chin to hide his clothes. The sound of running feet was heard from the stairs. They were now coming closer, down along the hall.

With a long leap, Frank reached his bed and dived in, alongside Barney.

Crash! The door was flung open and light pervaded the room.

The light showed four lads in bed, while everything seemed to be in order about the room. The fact that Cadet Hodge's clothes were not hanging in their proper place must have escaped the eyes of the inspector, for the door closed and the footsteps passed on.

"By me soul!" gasped Barney Mulloy, sitting up in bed. "But that was a close shave, boys!"

"That's right," agreed Ned Gray, also sitting up. "Say, Merriwell, you must have struck Hodge a fearful blow. He is awful still."

"I did strike him pretty hard," acknowledged Frank, "but I didn't think it would stun him like this."

"He doesn't stir," whispered Ned, in an awed way. "He doesn't even seem to breathe! I'm afraid he's hurt pretty bad."

Frank got up, his heart sinking. Already he was sorry for the blow, which had been delivered in the heat of Hodge's sudden assault, and the ominous silence of his enemy gave him a shivery feeling, as if his blood had congealed in his veins.

What if Hodge were seriously injured? What if that blow, delivered in self-defense, had broken the fellow's neck?

Such a thing was by no means an impossibility, and Frank Merriwell shuddered with horror as he thought what must follow in case it should be true.

There was nothing malicious or vicious in Frank's nature, and he had struck the blow purely in self-defense, without thinking of the possibility of serious consequences. Nor had it given him a single thrill of joy to know he had knocked Hodge out with a single punch, as he realized it was purely a matter of accident, and his blow might have been warded off or dodged had his enemy seen it coming.

Steadying his nerves, Frank got lightly out of bed,

and hurried to the side of the unconscious lad.

In truth Hodge lay ominously still. It was with no little reluctance that Merriwell felt for the fellow's heart, but a sigh of relief came from his lips when he felt that organ pulsating regularly beneath his hand.

"He will come round all right, I think," whispered Frank, as he gave the dark-haired lad a shake. "Come, come, Hodge, wake up."

Bart groaned a bit, and then caught his breath with a gasp, but made no effort to sit or stir.

"Bring me some water, Barney," directed Frank. "Be quiet. We don't want that fellow to come back here with the light."

The water was brought, and Merriwell used it to bathe Hodge's face and temples. This seemed to revive the stunned boy, who soon began to breathe regularly, and finally pushed Frank's hand away, muttering:

"Don't! It's wet."

"How do you feel, Hodge?" asked Ned Gray, who was still nervous. "Are you all right?"

"Feel? What do you mean? Of course I'm all right. What's happened, anyway?"

"Shh! Don't speak so loud, or you will be heard. You were struck, and ----"

"Struck? Who did it? I remember! Merriwell, he----"

"Tapped ya a dainty one, me laddybuck," chuckled Barney, who was delighted by the way things had turned out. "Between this and your other fight with him, I think ya will agree he is the best with his dukes."

Bart sat up, although it was an effort to do so, and there was a strange buzzing in his head.

"It was an accident," he savagely muttered.

"I could not see him, and I slipped. My head struck the floor, and dazed me. Merriwell is a good fighter---in the dark, where the other fellow can't see him,"

"Say, will you keep still!" hissed Ned, giving Bart a nudge. "You seem determined to get yourself and the rest of us into trouble tonight."

"I told him not to turn off the light."

"And you knew an inspecting officer would have been here in less than a minute if the light had not been off. It is Merriwell's place to see that it is out, and he would have suffered for it."

"Oh, you fellows are all against me!" snarled Bart, as he lay down again. "But I have friends. I will show you that I've got as many friends as Merriwell. We'll see who will stand ahead in this academy---we'll see!"

Frank had kept silent, glad to let the matter drop for the time being. He scarcely heard Bart's muttered words, and, being fatigued by the severe drilling through which he had passed that day, he soon fell asleep.

Twice Ned asked Bart if he did not intend to undress, but the fellow kept a sullen silence, and so Ned finally drifted away into the land of dreams, with Bart, still dressed, lying in the bed and outlining a hundred plots for vengeance on the boy he hated with a bitterness that seemed to increase with each passing moment.

Having a proud and sensitive nature, as well as a fierce temper, Bart felt humiliated and disgraced, and his bosom was full of the bitterest rancor. Over and over he told himself that he could kill Merriwell.

Bart's father was the richest man in the town where he resided, and Bart had been brought up in a way that usually spoils a boy. In his home he had been petted and indulged in every way, and in the village he had been something of a monarch among the boys, for he had spent money quite freely, and boys generally in the country are inclined to favor the fellow who has plenty of money.

In fact, Bart had been so indulged and spoiled that his father decided the only way to save him and make anything of him was to send him to a military school, where he would be forced to take his chances with the other boys, and would receive no favors.

From the first school to which Bart was sent, he wrote home the most pitiful and indignant letters, describing the "indignities" and "abuses" which he was compelled to suffer. His father smiled, and would have let the boy remain; but his mother raised such a ruckus that Mr. Hodge was finally forced to take his son out of the school.

Then Bart was sent to another academy, but this proved no better. Mr. Hodge, however, refused to take him out. For all of this, he did not remain long. He soon committed an act that brought about his expulsion.

By this time, Bart's father was thoroughly angry, and he made up his mind that the boy must remain at the next school to which he was sent. He expressed himself with decision and force to his wife and his son. To the latter, he said:

"Fardale Military Academy is said to be one of the best schools of the kind in the country. I am going to send you there, and you are going to stay there until you are ready for college. I shall not take you out on any condition, and, if you are expelled, you need not come back here looking for any further assistance from me. I shall send you out in the world to make your own living. That's it!"

Knowing his father as he did, Bart realized it was indeed final, and he had no desire to be expelled from Fardale Academy, although it seemed very humiliating to be forced to mingle with "ordinary fellows" and have no better things nor receive any more favors than he would if his father were barely able to pay his tuition.

Bart thought this all over as he lay there, and his heart was hot against his father for making him face the music in such a manner.

"Still, I believe I'd get along well if Merriwell got it in the neck," thought the musing lad. "If I could put up a job to get him expelled, I'd be quite happy and contented."

Thus thinking and plotting, he finally fell asleep.

He awoke to feel himself roughly shaken and heard a guarded whisper:

"Awake from thy slumber, plebe. Your presence is earnestly desired at a little matinee to be held immediately."

"Who are you? What do you want?" he sleepily asked.

A light from a dark lantern was flashed in his face.

"We are the Jolly Fiends of Fardale," replied a disguised voice, "and we want you."

The light was flashed round the room, and he saw it was filled with boys who wore masks over their faces!

CHAPTER XVII

NO ESCAPE

"Hazers!"

Bart gasped the word, sitting up suddenly. The light was flung upon him again, blinding him by its brightness, and he heard a laughing voice say:

"Behold, comrades! the chosen one is already dressed for the occasion."

Something like a hoarse chuckle ran round the room, sounding hollowly from behind the masks.

Ned awoke and turned over.

"What's the row now?" he asked, in a sleepy voice.

"Silence!" sternly commanded the leader of the Jolly Fiends. "If you speak louder than a whisper, may your doom be on your head."

"So mote it be!" came in a hushed and solemn murmur from the masked cadets.

"'Scuse me!" muttered Barney. "I'm not at home this evening." And with that, he ducked under his sheets.

Frank Merriwell was wide awake, but he kept still and said nothing, knowing that this was the best thing he could do.

But Merriwell was not to escape, having been selected for the "matinee" by the Jolly Fiends. Having discovered that he did not sleep next to Hodge, the leader said:

"Fellow-Fiends, our second victim must repose

on yonder cot. Cause him to arise and prepare to go forth with us."

In another moment, Frank was pounced upon and ordered to get up immediately and dress.

"All right, gentlemen," he said, with resignation. "But I trust you will allow me sufficient time to draw up my last will and testament before I am led forth to the slaughter?"

"Silence! If you are given time to say your prayers before standing face to face with your doom, you should be well satisfied. Arise."

"O.K. Arise it is."

Frank got out of bed quietly, and began to dress himself.

Bart, however, was not so willing to take his medicine.

"I will not get up! he declared. "I refuse to be hazed, and if you do not leave this room immediately I will----------"

"What?"

"I'll raise a rumpus that will arouse the whole academy."

"Oh, no you won't!" came grimly from the leader of the masks. "You will get up quietly, and take great care not to make enough noise to awaken anybody. I don't think you want to see your own brains scattered all over the wall, and this may bring you to realize that we are in deadly earnest."

Something bright and shiny showed in the speaker's steady hand, as the light flashed for a second upon it, and Hodge felt a cold muzzle pressed against his forehead. The touch gave him a thrill of fear, and he gasped:

"You---you wouldn't dare!"

"Wouldn't I?" was the deep, hoarse whisper that came back from the leader of the masks, who now seemed terribly in earnest. "I warn you not to force me into daring. I give you my word of honor that, as true as this weapon ever cracked a cartridge and sent a bullet with deadly force from its muzzle, I shall pull the trigger and it will plant another bullet in your head, if you raise a row. Take a tumble, and get up."

"This is an outrage! I will report it!"

"If you get troublesome, you may not find an opportunity to report it, sir. It is a sad thing for one like you to die so young."

"And so fair," murmured another voice.

"Hodge says it ain't fair at all at all," muttered Barney, who had ventured to peer out from beneath the sheets.

"I never before heard of such a dastardly outrage!" Bart grated. "The idea of using a gun to compel a fellow to take a hazing! It is criminal!"

"Be careful, sir!" warned the leader of the Jolly Fiends. "Every word you speak is noted and recorded and you will have to answer for it. Take warning!"

But Bart was too angry and too stubborn to be warned in such a manner.

"Old Gunn shall hear of this," he panted. "Some of you fellows will be expelled for this bit of work, mark what I say!"

"Yes," said the leader, "mark what he says-- mark it in the book of records, and let him answer for it on the day of judgment. Then there shall be weeping and wailing and gnashing of teeth, and great shall be the fall thereof, even though it be the spring of the year."

Bart was tempted to raise a shout, for all of that menacing weapon. But what if the revolver should be accidentally discharged? A shout might startle the fellow so he would press the trigger. A cold chill ran over the dark-haired boy, for

86

the muzzle of the terrible weapon kept steadily staring upon him. He grated his teeth, and then he started and shuddered again, for every one of those masked figures echoed the sound from behind the masks.

"There is not a false molar among them all," said the leader, cheerfully. "You should hear them crunching and snapping the bones of our last victim! Ah, it was sweet, sweet music! Methinks or methunks I can hear it even now."

"What rot!" exclaimed Bart, but he took care to speak softly. "You fellows are making blooming fools of yourselves!"

"But we will make a still more blooming fool of you," was the pleasant assurance. "Get up!"

"Well, I guess I can stand it if Merriwell can."

Hodge got up, and the hazers, who had really feared he would raise a rumpus, began to believe there was a possibility that they would carry out their plot successfully.

"Remove those shoes from thy pedal extremities," directed the leader.

Bart obeyed.

By this time, Frank was sufficiently dressed, and one of the masked fellows slowly and gently raised the window. Then he thrust out his head for the purpose of making an inspection.

"The coast is clear," he quickly declared, drawing back and securing the window. "I will go ahead."

Then he climbed over the sill, swung down by his hands, and dropped. As the room was on the second story, he did not have far to fall, and he landed lightly, like a cat, upon his feet. A second and a third followed, and then Merriwell was ordered to make the drop.

Frank did not hold back. As quietly as he could, he got out over the sill, and hung by his hands. Then, pushing himself out a bit from the wall with his knee, he let go and dropped, doing the trick as skillfully as the others had done.

Then came three more wearers of masks, and Hodge followed them. He made some noise in getting through the window, but was warned again by the leader, who stood beside him, with the terrible weapon ready for instant use.

When Hodge had made the drop, the leader of the Jolly Fiends turned to two of his masked companions, saying:

"You are to stay and keep guard over the plebes here. When you hear the signal, let down the knotted rope for us. It is not likely we shall be back inside of two hours."

"Correct, your royal muchness," was the reply. "We will look after these two plebes. But what if they attempt to kick up a racket?"

"Beat out their brains with the pillows on these beds," was the order. "Those pillows are far more deadly than this revolver in my hand. A blow from one of them is enough to shatter the strongest constitution. Farewell."

Then he crept out through the window and dropped.

On striking the ground he found himself quite alone, but that did not seem to surprise him. He had his shoes in his hand almost as soon as he struck the ground, as they had been concealed about his person all the time, and he quickly darted round to the back of the academy, scudded under the shadow of the tall elm trees, and was soon with the little band who were putting on their shoes by the guardhouse.

Hodge's and Merriwell's shoes had been brought along, and they were putting them on. Hodge was still growling about the outrage of forcing a fellow to be hazed at the muzzle of a revolver.

"You talk a great deal with your mouth, young man!" said the leader of the masks, in disgust. "Here, take a good look at that deadly revolver!"

Someone produced the dark lantern and flashed the light upon the weapon, which the speaker had produced from one of his pockets.

Hodge gave a gasp of surprise and disgust as he saw what lay in the open hand of the leader of the Jolly Fiends.

It was simply a nickel-covered water-faucet, such as are in common use on water pipes!

CHAPTER XVIII

HANS SINGS A SONG

A groan came from Bart Hodge's lips, and, had they not been so near the academy, the boys would have roared with laughter. It was a joke that everyone but Hodge thoroughly enjoyed.

"I--I don't believe it," he said, weakly. "I don't believe that was the weapon you held a-gainst my head. I heard you cock it--I heard it click."

"You have a very vivid imagination, sir," said the leader of the masks, as he restored the faucet to his pocket and continued putting on his shoes. "I assure you that you are mistaken."

"If I had known, I'd--I'd--"

"What?"

"I'd raised such a rumpus that you wouldn't have worked your little racket so far. By thunder, I'm going to do it now! I'll shout---"

"If you do," came sternly from the leader of the Fiends, "I will agree to see that you receive the worst hammering you ever ran up against in all your life. We'll all get a crack at you, and you will not look very pretty in the morning. Eh, boys?"

"Correct, your royal muchness," came from every one of the masked faces.

Bart hesitated. He did not relish the idea of being pounded by a group of masked fellows whom he did not know. If he had known them all, so he might report them, he would have set up a shout without delay. As it was, he said:

"Oh, well, you've got me here, and I suppose I may as well see the matter through; but I give you fair warning that you want to be careful what you do to me."

"Oh, yes, we'll be careful!" came from several of the cadets, and the way they spoke the words gave Bart a very shivery feeling.

In a few moments all had their shoes on, and then, following the leader, they slipped across the grounds, keeping beneath the shadows of the trees and close to the walls of the buildings, skirted the plain, and finally reached the limit of the grounds without being seen.

"Where are you taking me?" asked Bart.

"Keep still, and you will find out," was the sharp reply.

Leaving the grounds, they proceeded with less caution, but still maintaining silence. They came to the shore of the cove on which the academy was located, and this they followed for at least half a mile.

Finally a private boathouse was reached. From within came the sounds of boisterous merriment, as if a great collection of young fellows had assembled within, and Bart suddenly grew desperate, resolving to make a break for liberty, rather than go in there.

It seemed as if his very thoughts were surmised, for hands were placed firmly on his arms, and he found he could not get away if he wished, so he gave up the desperate project.

A peculiar rap on the door of the boathouse caused the merriment within to be hushed quickly. The rap was repeated, and then the door opened.

"Enter," ordered the leader of the Jolly Fiends, and Bart was forced to march in.

Frank followed quietly.

The boathouse seemed swarming with masked lads, and the cause of their merriment soon became apparent, for Hans Dunnerwust was there, his fat face painted like that of a wild Indian about to take to the warpath, and his hair filled full of feathers which looked as if they had been plucked from the tails of half-a-dozen different roosters. With a wooden tomahawk and scalping knife in his hands, he had just finished a wild war dance that had quite put him out of breath, and he was puffing and gasping in the middle of the floor.

The appearance of Hodge and Merriwell was hailed with a shout of delight from the masked cadets assembled in the boathouse, and they all began to sing:

"We'll give them the rink of the blinkety-blink,
    And crush their weak bones, ker-chunk;
We'll give them the spank of the blankety-blank,
    And laugh at their moans, ker-plunk."

"Ker-chunk" and "ker-plunk" at the end of the second and fourth lines were brought out with great emphasis. Immediately, as if by mutual understanding, the song changed to this:

"Let us all unite in love,
While Old Gunn's asleep above;
Let us all unite in love,
And give these plebes a gentle shove.

"In the neck, in the neck they will get it,
In the neck, in the neck, where it fits;
If you laugh when they squeal, you will hit it,
For they'll get it in the neck, where it fits."

The door closed behind the new delegation and their victims, being securely fastened.

Hans Dunnerwust gave a sigh of relief as he saw Frank and Bart.

"Vell, maybe I vas clad you have come!" he exclaimed. "Maybe dese fellers a rest vill give me now, ya?"

But Hans was not to escape yet.

"You haven't taken your third degree, Cadet Dunnerwust," said the master of ceremonies. "Nor have you sung that song we desire to hear so very much."

"Vell, didn't I tell you that I didn't know how to sing very good?"

"You are altogether too modest, sir. I am sure that anyone with such a musical voice as yours can sing divinely. Take your place in the center of the room there, and begin at once."

Hans stood helplessly on the spot indicated, but he was the picture of despair as he looked all around.

"Vat shall I zing?" he asked.

"You might carol that tender little ditty entitled 'Who Threw Mush in Willie's Eye?'" suggested one.

"I don't know that one."

"Then you may warble 'He Had a Little Eyebrow Growing on His Lip.'"

"I don't know that one."

"Is it possible! I fear your musical education has been sadly neglected. Give us a few stanzas of 'How He Rambled Through His Brother's Appetite.'"

"Vell, I don't know that one, either."

"This is sincerely distressing," sighed the leader. "What can you sing?"

"Vell, I have heard dat zong called 'Bull for der Shore.'"

"Very well; you may give us 'Bull for der Shore.'"

"Vait a minute until I think of it. It has been more than a veek since I heard it for der last time."

Hans scratched his head and looked puzzled, but finally grinned and announced:

"I have it."

Then he took in a deep breath, threw back his head, and began to sing, in the most discordant manner imaginable:

"Bull for der shore, sailor, bull for der shore,
Get inter dat lifeboat, and get off der roof,
Spit on your hands, sailor, and let her rip,
If you don't brace up, you get left already yet.''

There was something so ludicrous about Hans' effort to sing and the manner in which he had twisted the words of the hymn about that the listeners, with the exception of Bart, roared with laughter.

Frank was actually enjoying every minute of the time, and he had enjoyed it since the appearance of the masked cadets in his room at the barracks. He had made up his mind to take what might come and make as little fuss about it as possible, and he did not worry over what was in store for himself.

On the other hand, while Bart would have enjoyed it hugely had he been one of the hazers, he felt that he was humiliated in the eyes of his companions, and that cut his sensitive spirit keenly, so, under the circumstances, he did not enjoy it at all.

Hans stopped singing, and twenty voices shouted:

"Go on, sir--go on!"

"But I don't know any more of dat zong."

"Sing it over again."

With a sickly grin, the Dutch boy did as directed.

"Louder! louder!" was the cry.

So he sang louder, and he was told to keep singing it over and over until directed to stop.

"Louder! louder!" shouted the masked boys.

Hans shut both eyes tightly, and opened his mouth to its greatest capacity, and roared out the words as loudly as he could. He was repeating the stanza for the sixth time when something happened.

Spat! A rotten apple, flung by an unerring hand, struck the Dutch boy fairly in the mouth.

The song ended very abruptly.

CHAPTER XIX

GHOSTLY SOUNDS

The decayed apple came near choking the unfortunate boy to death; and it caused him to spit and sputter and gurgle in a most distressing manner. Some of it was spattered over his painted face, and he presented a most pitiful spectacle.

"Guten Himmel!" he gurgled. "Vat vas dat? It tasted like it has been exposed to injury already yet."

The way he uttered the words threw the cadets into convulsions. The boathouse rang with their shouts of laughter.

"This is a disgrace!" grated Bart. "It shall be reported to Professor Gunn."

"I presume you will report it?" said one of the masked Fiends.

"That I will," was the ready assurance.

Immediately Bart's words were repeated so that all those assembled could hear them, and Bart found that he had drawn an unenviable amount of attention on himself.

"I think we will give Cadet Dunnerwust a rest, and devote some of our valuable time and attention to Cadet Hodge," observed the master of ceremonies. "By his language, just quoted, it is evident that he looks upon our noble order with disfavor. What shall be done with him?"

"Run him through the mill!" roared more than a score of voices.

Instantly Bart was seized and hustled in a manner that bewildered him and took away his breath. From side to side he was tossed, and when he stumbled and would have fallen, he was caught up and kept moving. He tried to strike out in defense, but his blows encountered nothing but air. His teeth were clenched and his eyes blazed with unutterable fury, yet he found himself utterly helpless in the hands of the masked boys.

"Oh, you'll be sorry for this!" he panted.

Then, when he was so weak that his legs threatened to give way beneath him, they caught him up, and, before he could comprehend their scheme, he found himself on his back on a piece of sailcloth. Around the sailcloth stood a circle of boys who grasped the edges.

"Bounce him!" commanded a voice, and Bart was tossed, writhing and kicking, into the air.

Down he came on the sailcloth, and up he went again, before he could get his breath. Again and again, he went higher with each toss, until he touched the rafters away up toward the roof. His head swam, and the breath seemed torn and jounced from his lips. A feeling of nausea seized him, and still that terrible tossing went on.

When it was over, Bart was too weak to stand, and much of his spirit had been taken out of him for the time being, at least. He was pale about the mouth, and he sank in a nerveless heap to the floor.

"Give him a few moments to get his breath," said the leader. "We'll take a whirl at the other victim now."

Frank knew it was his turn.

"What have you to say about it, Mr. Merriwell?" he was asked.

"Not a word," was the quiet reply.

"I suppose you mean to report this affair

to Old Gunn."

"Not if I can help it," was the reply. "I am not in the habit of telling things when the joke is on me."

"Do you mean that you won't tell?"

"Not unless I have to."

"He's saying that so you will go light with him," came husikly from Bart. "That's his little game."

"Well, he has made an error in that case," said the leader. "We never let up on anybody. The fellow who gets into Fardale and stays here has to take the regular course, no matter who he is."

Bart laughed, sneeringly:

"It didn't work, did it, Merriwell!" he cried.

At that moment, apparently just outside the door, a dog began to bark loudly. The boys looked startled.

"Wonder whose dog that is?" speculated one. "Can it be somebody is prowling around here?"

"The sentries have given us no warning."

"That must be a stray dog. Somebody drive him away."

The door was opened, and the barking ceased, but not a sign of a dog could be found.

"Well, he scudded away quick," said the boy who had started to drive him away.

He closed the door, and barely had he done so when the dog gave a most dismal and mournful howl.

Quick as a flash, he flung the door open and jumped out, but not a sign of the creature supposed to be close outside could he discover, and he re-entered in a minute, looking all around the room, and showing by his manner that he was puzzled.

The instant the door was closed that mysterious howling burst forth again.

The boys looked from one to another in dismay.

"What in thunder is the meaning of it?" muttered one. "It has a ghostly sound."

"That's so," nodded another. "And that makes me think of the story about old Jake Henderson being murdered in this very place. His dog stayed by the body and howled until somebody came. When Henderson was buried, the dog stayed by the grave night and day, and howled himself to death.

"Perhaps that is the ghost of Henderson's dog that we hear howling outside."

The suggestion caused more than one to shiver, and the laugh that followed the words was not a very hearty one.

"Who believes in ghosts!" cried one lad, derisively. "That's all rot! I'm not afraid --- What's that?"

They listened, and the sound was repeated --- a hollow, awful groan. Where it came from no one seemed able to tell.

"Holy Moses!" gurgled the fellow who had just declared he was not afraid of ghosts. "I don't exactly like the sound of that."

The way he said this, and the change in his manner, brought a burst of laughter from the boys, but they hushed quickly when the groan again echoed hollowly through the room.

"Jupiter!" said a tall boy. "I believe it comes from the roof."

"And I think it cuc-cuc-cuc-comes from under the fuf-fuf-fuf-floor," chattered a short boy.

"Listen!"

"I cannot rest! I cannot rest! The grave is dark and cold."

All heard the words distinctly, and more than one felt his hair trying to stand erect on his head.

"Great Jupiter!" whispered an unsteady voice, distinctly heard in the hush that followed. "I guess it is old Henderson's ghost for sure, boys!"

"Not much!" stoutly declared the leader of the hazers. "Henderson was most illiterate. He never said 'cannot' in all his life. He would have said 'can't rest.'"

"Perhaps he has been studying grammar since his departure from this mundane sphere," suggested another fellow.

"Someone is trying to work a joke on us," said the leader, with decision. "I am sure of it. Six of you follow me lively, and we will see if we can't catch the guy."

Out of the door he dashed, and he was quickly followed by the required number, while the rest remained and discussed Henderson's murder and ghosts in general.

Frank Merriwell was taking things easy, quite satisfied by his success in diverting attention from himself for the time, for it was he who had, by the aid of his ventriloquial powers, produced all the mysterious sounds that had been heard. He had known nothing of the murder of Henderson and the devotion of the murdered man's dog. It was quite by chance that he had chosen to make it seem that a dog was howling at the door of the boathouse. The talk that had followed between the Jolly Friends had given him his cue to work upon, and he had succeeded to his complete satisfaction.

"What's the use of being hazed, if you can't have some fun at the same time?" thought Frank.

The party who had gone outside were absent nearly ten minutes before they returned, looking disgusted and baffled.

"What did you find?" was the question that greeted them.

"Not a thing," they replied. "There's no one anywhere around outside."

"But we heard the voice distinctly, and the dog—"

From just beyond the door, a long-drawn howl of agony seemed to proceed from the throat of the mysterious dog.

"Howl, confound you!" grated the leader of the Jolly Fiends. "You can't howl enough to scare me away! I'm going to stay right here until these plebes are put through the entire course of sprouts. That's the kind of fellow I am."

"And I am going to see what your face looks like!" shouted Bart Hodge. "That's the kind of a fellow I am!"

With a panther-like spring, he reached a position where he could snatch the mask from the leader's face, and this he accomplished with astonishing swiftness.

The face revealed was that of Walter Burrage, corporal of cadets!

CHAPTER XX

BURRAGE IN A BAD FIX

"You are a very good-looking fellow, sneered the triumphant Bart, "but this night's work will cost you your chevrons, if it does not cause you to be expelled from Fardale Academy. Oh, you won't put on so many airs after this!"

Burrage was pale and not a little frightened, for he realized it would be a very serious thing for him if Hodge really squealed to Professor Gunn. He saw he was in a bad scrape, for Bart was just the little kind of a fellow to report the whole matter, and he was the sort of a boy who could not be easily frightened out of anything he had made up his mind to do.

Frank was sorry for Burrage, but that did not help the matter any.

"Look here, Mr. Hodge," said the unmasked hazer, "I hope you do not mean that you really intend to squeal?"

"Well, you can bet your life I do mean it! Do you think I am the kind of a fellow to be run through the mill and not take an opportunity to get square?"

"I thought it possible you might not wish to get every cadet in the academy down on you, as they certainly will be if you report this matter to Professor Gunn."

"That kind of a bluff won't go with me," was Bart's haughty retort. "I didn't come to Fardale to be made a monkey of, and I am going to stand up for my rights.''

"You will find you have no easy life to live here, if you begin by squealing.''

Bart snapped his fingers in Burrage's face.

"I tell you the bluff won't go with me. I've got you now, and I'll pay you back for dragging me out of my bed and bringing me here to have sport with. If the other fellows who come here and are hazed would show a little more spirit and squeal occasionally, I fancy the Jolly Fiends would soon cease to exist.''

Burrage was desperate. Hodge had insulted him by words and manner, but he could not afford to resent it, although the hot blood had flushed the cheeks that were very pale a few seconds before. He turned appealingly to Merriwell:

"You will agree not to squeal, won't you, Merriwell?'' he asked.

"Sure,'' replied Frank, cheerily. "You are welcome to all the fun you have had with me. Any time you want to haze me it isn't necessary to put on masks. Just send me a notification, and I will meet you anywhere. I'm one of the most accommodating fellows you ever saw.''

"Three cheers for Merriwell!'' shouted one of the throng, and the cheers were given.

That angered Bart more than anything else could have done.

"Oh, Merriwell knows how to work his cards!'' he sneered. "He is playing it very smooth.''

"You can't prove anything without his aid, for your word is no better than mine,'' said Burrage.

"Is that so? I rather think you have forgotten the other fellow who has suffered at your hands tonight.''

"Dunnerwust?''

"Exactly. He will substantiate me.''

"I don't know vat that means," said Hans, "but I bet mein life that I don't do it."

"They have imposed on you shamefully, Dunnerwust," said Hodge. "I want you to go with me to Professor Gunn and tell just what has happened, and state that Mr. Burrage here, whose mask I removed, was the leader."

Hans listened with his mouth open, a stolid look on his fantastically painted face.

"You vant me to do dat, hey?" he said.

"Yes."

"Vell, I von't."

"What?"

"I'm not that kind of a person," declared the Dutch boy, much to the amazement of everyone. "Dose fellers raised particular fits mit me, and I think I laughed through them just like they did. Vat for should I squeal to the professor? By me, ven I gets to be a big gun mit der rest of the boys, I vas goin' to have fun mit some other plebes. You can substantiate all you vans to, but you don't get Hans Dunnerwust to do some of dat mit you."

"Hurrah for Dunnerwust!" was the cry, and Hans was given a rousing ovation.

The boys had not counted on anything of this kind from the Dutch boy. Burrage had thought it possible he might frighten Hans into keeping still, in case he could induce Hodge to be silent.

The stand Hans took should have shamed Hodge, but it did not seem to affect him any further than to make him angry.

"You're a bigger fool than I thought you were!" he exclaimed, savagely. "I don't believe you know enough to come in when it rains!"

"Dat's all right too. You vas velcome to think vat you please, and I do der same mit you. If I vas a blamed fool, I don't be any sneak."

103

"Good stuff! roared the boys. "We'll swear by you after this, Dutchy."

"You see, Hodge," said Burrage, "you will be alone in this matter if you report it. Neither Merriwell nor Dunnerwust will help you, ---"

"I'll tell what happened, and they will have to tell the truth or a lie, in case they are questioned."

What course of "persuasion" Burrage would have resorted to cannot be told, for at this moment there came the sound of hurrying feet outside, and a sharp, peculiar rap on the door.

"The danger signal!" cried the unmasked cadet, leaping to the door. "Out with the lights, fellows!"

The order was obeyed, and the interior of the boathouse was plunged into darkness.

Burrage flung open the door, hastily asking: "What's up?"

"There's some stirring in the academy," was the panted reply. "It is likely an inspection of rooms is going on."

"Then some of the profs must have got wind of something," said Burrage. "We'll have to hustle in, fellows, and trust to luck to get into our beds without detection."

There was a general scurrying out of the boathouse, but Burrage waited quietly for Hodge. When Bart appeared, the exposed cadet tackled him again, telling the others to leave them.

Exactly what passed between Hodge and Burrage nobody but themselves could have told, but they reached the academy almost as soon as most of the others, and Burrage whispered to a companion that Bart would not squeal first thing in the morning.

At the signal agreed upon, certain windows of the academy opened, and knotted ropes were let down to the boys, most of whom showed a skill in climbing that betokened considerable experience.

Much to their relief, the boys found everything quiet about the academy, and, one by one, they climbed the ropes and stole away to their rooms.

Hans Dunnerwust was the last to make the attempt to get up the rope, and, after he had fallen back three times, it became necessary to have him tie it about his body under the arms, so the boys above could pull him up into the window.

"It must have been a false alarm," thought Frank, when he found himself safely in his room, with no sign of anyone moving about the academy besides the cadets who had just slipped in.

He undressed quietly, and got into bed, Hodge doing the same. No words passed between them.

"Burrage surely is in a bad scrape," thought Merriwell, "for Hodge will try to strike a blow at Inza by having her brother disgraced. I would do anything for her, and I wish there were some way I could save the fellow."

But, although he lay awake thinking of the matter for a long time, he could not seem to devise any scheme for Burrage's rescue.

Yet Burrage was to be saved at the cost of more than one heart pang for Frank.

CHAPTER XXI

A SURPRISE FOR FRANK

It was generally conceded by the boys at the academy that Burrage was in a "mighty bad box," for it seemed certain that Hodge would report him to Old Gunn, in which case demerit and loss of chevrons must follow, even if nothing of a more serious nature resulted.

Burrage had won his position at the school by hard, persistent work, and he was regarded generally as deserving of the stripes. He had taken an active interest in all kinds of sports and games, being captain of both the baseball team and the football team, and he would be missed severely if he were expelled.

"Hodge will never be able to stay in this academy if he drives Burrage out," said more than one.

There was a slight feeling of relief when the first forenoon passed after the events of the previous night at the boathouse, and Burrage was not called to account. Still the suspense continued, for no one could tell when the blow would fall.

Some of the cadets tried to get Hodge aside and "have a hack" at him, but he craftily avoided anything of the kind, seeming well satisfied with the attention he was receiving just then.

"These fellows are beginning to realize that I count at this school, that is plain," he chuckled to himself. "If I can get two or three more of the high and mighty ones under my thumb, it is possible they will not be so very lofty and overbearing."

Hodge was impatient to receive his uniform and be assigned.

"I do not think much of this herding four in a room," he declared, in the presence of his roommates. "I am not used to it, and it goes against my grain."

"Have your talk with Cle Gunn and it's likely he'll give ya a room all by yerself," said Barney Mulloy. "And if he does, ya'll never be missed at all."

"You're altogether too free with your lip, Mulloy!" snapped the dark-eyed boy. "You should be a little more respectful when addressing your betters."

"I am, boy; but you're not on the list."

That was too much for Bart's fiery temper.

"You and Merriwell make a good pair!" he flashed. "He is just the sort of a fellow to bunk with a common Irishman."

Now Barney had a temper of his own, for all that he was usually jovial and light-hearted, and this was too much for him. He made a rush at Hodge, and there would have been trouble instantly had not both Frank and Ned intervened.

"Don't mind him," said Merriwell. "It is not likely we will all be in one room many days longer, and ---"

"That's right," cut in Bart. "Nor will we be in one company. I have a lap on you fellows, for I have seen military schools before, and I am sure of being assigned to the first squad."

"Oh you are, well then I hope I'm in the last," muttered Barney. "I want to be as far from ya as possible."

Hodge was really confident that his knowledge of drill work would place him in the first squad, for all that the system at Fardale, copied after that in vogue at West Point, was much more rigid and difficult than anything he had previously encountered.

At many military schools in this country the strictly business system of instruction insisted on by soldiers is set aside for something of a showy nature, but also utterly useless except for the purpose of display.

Now it so happened that Hodge's previous experience had been at such schools, and, instead of helping him on, as he expected, what he had already learned held him back, for he was forced to unlearn it and acquire something entirely different and at variance.

Repeatedly, he declared the system at Fardale was entirely wrong, and it did not change his view in this respect at all to be assured that the entire manual was an accurate copy of the one at West Point. Such being the case, Bart declared that West Point must be old-fogyish and behind the times.

Oh, the infinitely superior wisdom of some youngsters!

For the new boys at Fardale Academy the first days were wretched and exasperating. It was a case of drill, drill, drill all the time, with scarcely any let-up. It seemed that the yearlings who had them in charge took a fiendish delight in working them to the verge of endurance. They were forced to keep twisting, turning, bending and extending for hours, and in this way their muscles were sore and stiffened at first, and their very bones seemed to grow lame. Still those heartless yearlings kept them at it, rising on tiptoe, bending double, springing up, swaying forward, backward, and sideways, working, working, working, and never seeming to get any rest.

It did not take much of this to convince the boys that they had two or three thousand sore muscles in their body of which no mention could be found in physiology.

What did it amount to? Why, after a while the soreness began to wear off, and they found that they could go through the evolutions, convolutions, and revolutions much easier and more swiftly. The awkward squad developed into youths worthy to receive uniforms.

The whole school seemed to breathe easier as time slipped away and Hodge still remained silent concerning his experiences at the boathouse. For two or three days, while the suspense continued, the plebes surely had a much easier time of it at the hands of their cadet instructors.

"Burrage must have fixed it up some way with Hodge," was the final decision. "Either that, or Hodge is not so bad a fellow as he seemed."

Both Burrage and Hodge kept silent about the matter, and it proved useless to question them.

By his roommates Hodge was seen smiling over a dainty letter he had received. The stationery was distinctly feminine, as was the writing upon the envelope, which the fellow took good care to display.

Merriwell avoided Hodge as much as possible. He had at last decided that Bart was a churl, and he did not wish to have anything to do with such a person. Knowing that he could not endure much of Hodge's insolence, he tried to give his foe little opportunity to be insulting.

All through his first week at the academy, Frank had longed for Saturday to arrive, as he had been invited to call on Inza Burrage on the afternoon of that day. He anticipated a most pleasant call, well knowing how welcome he would be in the eyes of the girl's parents, who regarded the savior of their daughter from the fangs of a rabid dog as a young knight of modern times.

The day came around at last, and Frank dressed himself in his best, taking the greatest pains to note that his linen was immaculate, his tie tastily tied, his clothes brushed, his shoes polished, and his soft hat crushed with a careless air. He spent a long time before the mirror.

Hodge left the academy nearly an hour before Frank, and he was also dressed in his best, although his taste ran to the flashy, and he did not display anything like Merriwell's good taste.

Having passed outside of the beautiful grounds that surrounded the academy, Frank stepped off briskly toward Fardale, whistling a cheery tune. It was a bright , sunshiny afternoon, and he was in high spirits. At times he could not restrain the boyish inclination to hop, but he made sure he was out of sight of the academy before indulging in any such antics.

Reaching the quiet little village, he walked along the tree-shaded streets until he came to Inza Burrage's home. A handsome carriage and a spirited, well-groomed horse stood in front of the house. A boy was holding the horse.

Barely giving this turn-out a glance, Frank ran up the steps and rang the bell.

After a brief delay, a maid appeared at the door.

"Is Miss Burrage at home?" asked Frank.

"She is," was the reply.

"Please give her my card."

He placed a neat card in the maid's fingers, at the same time stepping into the hall. To his surprise, he was requested to wait there.

"Well, this is an odd reception," he thought, as he stood stiffly in the hall, awaiting the return of the maid.

The young woman was not gone long. In a very brief space of time she returned, and said:

"Miss Inza begs to be excused today. She has callers at present, and cannot see you."

"Cannot see me?" repeated Frank, rather dazed.

"No, sir."

He seemed stunned as he turned away. Nothing in the world could have been more unexpected than this. She had invited him to call, and now she declined to see him. What did it mean?

He stepped out of the door and heard it close behind him. For a moment he stood irresolutely on the step, beginning to believe it was all a mistake. She had not refused to see him--it was not possible. For a moment he was tempted to ring the bell again and demand to receive further assurance that Miss Burrage would not see him; then he realized what a breach of propriety that would be, and he slowly descended the steps. As he did so, he fancied he heard someone laugh within the parlor.

The laugh sounded as if it came from the lips of Bartley Hodge!

CHAPTER XXII

CUT !

The boy who was holding the horse grinned as Frank reached the sidewalk and turned away. The urchin seemed to suspect or know the truth.

"Refused to see me!" muttered Frank, as he turned away, without casting a look back. "Who would have thought such a thing possible! But it is like a girl!" he added, bitterly. "They are all changeable and fickle!"

Had he glanced back he would have been further humiliated by seeing Bart smiling triumphantly at him from one of the parlor windows.

For some time he walked along like one dazed, paying little heed to his surroundings. Finally he aroused himself with a start, gave himself a shake, and said:

"I'll be hanged if I will make a fool of myself over any girl! I will show Miss Burrage that I am not all broken up."

Feeling the necessity of action, exercise, something to stir him up and make him forget what had just taken place, he inquired the way to the nearest livery stable, where he asked for the best saddle horse to be obtained.

"I want one with plenty of life and spirit," he said.

"There's one with plenty of life and spirit," said the hostler, indicating a handsome black gelding in a box stall; "but you can't ride him."

"Why not?"

"Can't handle him."

That aroused Frank, for he was a most expert horseman, and he had broken more than one vicious animal.

"I want that horse."

"Why, you are crazy!" cried the hostler. "There is but one man in Fardale who can ride him."

"If there is one, that is quite enough. Can you put the saddle on him, or shall I?"

"I can saddle him, but I won't let a young fellow like you have him. I'm not going to murder you!"

"Where is the proprietor?"

"What do you want?"

"I want that horse, and I am going to have him, if money will hire him."

The proprietor happened to be in the office, and, hearing these words, he came out. When he looked Frank over, he shook his head, saying:

"I don't dare let you have that horse, young man. He will throw you as fast as you can get into the saddle."

"If he throws me once, I'll agree not to make another attempt to ride him, and I will pay you ten dollars for the privilege of getting into the saddle. Here is the money, which I will deposit with you now, with the understanding that it is yours if he throws me once, and you are to take the regular pay for the use of him in case I succeed in riding him."

The man looked at the bright new ten-dollar bill and hesitated. Finally he took the money, and said:

"All right, young fellow, you may try your luck; but I have warned you, and I will not be held responsible. I hope he will not kill you when he throws you."

At first glance Frank had seen that the horse was not a vicious beast. The animal had not been broken properly, and, having thrown almost everyone who had attempted to ride him, he felt it his duty to keep it up.

Had the creature been vicious, he would not have permitted the hostler to strap on the saddle with scarcely any trouble.

Frank was not dressed for riding, but in his present state of mind, he did not mind that. He wanted something to take up his mind and make him forget what had just happened, and he was eager for the struggle with the horse.

When the saddle was properly adjusted and everything was ready, Frank procured a riding whip and prepared to mount. The horse turned its head, and watched him suspiciously out of the corner of its eye.

"I'll try to hold him until you get into the saddle," said the hostler, keeping at the bit.

Frank smiled, for he saw the man was frightened.

"You needn't bother to hold him," he said. "Give me the bit, and stand aside."

He took the horse by the bit, but did not waste a moment in attempting to soothe or fondle the creature. The hostler and the proprietor were astounded to see him give the bit a wrench that sat the animal back on its haunches, and then, before the beast could recover, he was on its back. When the horse lunged to its feet Frank Merriwell was sitting securely in the saddle.

With a wild squeal, the animal shot like a rocket out of the stable.

A number of the villagers had gathered about to see the fun. Some were grinning in expectation, and some were saying it was a shame to let the boy risk his life in such a manner, while yet others declared Frank a fool and rather hoped he would be seriously injured.

At two leaps the black gelding cleared the stable

114

and reached the center of the road, where he stopped with his forward feet braced and his back humped, his head going down. Everybody expected to see the boy shoot out of the saddle and fly headlong to the ground, but nothing of the kind occurred. As if glued to the horse, Frank remained securely in the saddle.

Probably nobody was more astonished than was the horse. The creature had expected to unseat Frank at the first effort, but, instead of that, it felt itself soundly cut by the whip, while the strange youth still remained securely and firmly on its back.

Again a wild squeal came from the horse, and then the staring villagers saw a battle royal between the boy and beast, for the creature did everything possible to unseat Frank without lying down and rolling over, but the boy would not be shaken, and the whip continued to score the glossy hide of the obstinate animal.

It took several minutes of this to convince the horse that it had met its master, and then, of a sudden, the creature gave in.

The crowd cheered admiringly as the boy rode away in triumph, now speaking soothingly to the excited horse, and stroking its neck.

This battle had sent Frank's blood leaping in his veins, and, for the time, he entirely forgot Inza Burrage and her refusal to see him.

Not for long, however.

He had finally gotten the splendid horse fully under control and quieted down when he observed coming toward him the very horse he had seen the boy holding in front of Inza's house.

In the carriage sat Inza herself, with Bart Hodge triumphantly driving at her side.

Frank paled, and the hot blood poured to his cheeks. A feeling of bitter anger and resentment swept over him.

So this was why she had refused to see him! She

had forgotten the past, and once more accepted Bart Hodge in preference to him! Had there been a side street near, he would have wheeled into it, and thus escaped meeting them, but there was nothing of the sort, and he could not make up his mind to turn squarely about before their very faces.

"I'll have to face it out!" he grated, through his teeth.

Now, Frank Merriwell was too much the gentleman to openly show resentment, so, when the carriage came near, he lifted his hat with all the grace and courtesy he could command.

Inza Burrage gave him a flitting glance, her face quite pale, and coldly turned away.

She had publicly cut him!

Bart Hodge grinned sneeringly, and the carriage rolled past.

All the angry color fled from Frank Merriwell's cheeks, and he turned pale once more. This was almost more than he could endure, and it was by exercising the utmost of his self-control that he held himself in check at that moment.

What followed during the next hour afterward seemed something like a dream to him. He remembered that he lashed the horse unmercifully, and rode at a mad gallop, somewhere, anywhere. His brain seemed in a tumult, and, for the first time in his life, he felt that he had an enemy whom he would rejoice to strangle. Had he met Bart Hodge alone in the open country while in this mood, a serious encounter must have taken place between them.

At length the cool breeze fanned his cheeks until he became calmer, and he turned back along a new road that led toward the village.

He felt that he desired never to see Inza again. He could feel nothing but scorn and contempt for a girl who would thus treat one who had saved her life at the risk of his own.

116

And he made up his mind that he would strangle Hodge if the fellow ever spoke of the matter in his presence. Growing calmer and calmer, he rode on until the village was close at hand.

Far away along the railroad he heard the whistle of the afternoon express, which did not stop at Fardale, but went whizzing through at top speed. The train was in sight when he was startled to hear a faint clatter of hoofs, the rattle of wheels, and a feminine scream of terror.

The voice was that of a girl he knew very well-- Inza!

CHAPTER XXIII

SAVED !

Parallel with the road along which Frank Merriwell was riding ran another road, and, just as the railroad was reached, the two roads united like the upper forks of a great Y, only they came together with a sweep, like the bottom of the letter U.

Down this other road a runaway horse was plunging, dragging a rocking, swaying carriage, in which were clinging two persons.

It was the team Bart had hired at the village livery stable, and the occupants of the carriage were Bart and Inza.

The horse had become frightened and unmanageable, and Hodge had lost his head and control of the animal, which was carrying him and his companion straight toward the railroad crossing.

Frank saw all this at a glance, and he saw that a terrible catastrophe seemed almost sure to take place. One swift look had told him that the runaway would reach the crossing at nearly the same instant the engine of the express went whizzing by.

"They will be killed!" gasped the boy on the black gelding.

And then, in the twinkling of an eye, he flew to action.

With his whip he cut the horse he bestrode, and sent the creature straight at the fence at one side of the road.

The spirited horse rode directly to the structure, clearing it in a manner that would have filled Frank with admiration under other circumstances.

Across the narrow field that separated the two forks of the road he cut at an angle that was intended to intercept the runaway.

Bart saw the terrible peril that menaced himself and his fair companion, and he sawed madly at the reins, but without avail, as the runaway had the bit in its teeth and would not be stopped.

The engineer of the express, from a distance, saw the runaway, and the engine whistle sent out a frantic signal of "down breaks."

"They can't stop!" muttered the boy on the horse. "It is impossible!"

Cut! cut! cut! went the whip, and the handsome horse fairly flew across the field.

Frank's heart was in his mouth.

"How can I save them? How can I save them?" he kept asking himself. "The runaway horse will be too near the crossing for me to stop him. How can I save them?"

And then he witnessed an act that made his blood boil with indignation.

Finding he could not stop the horse, and seeing the animal was almost certain to reach the crossing just in time to be hurled to death, Bart rose in the wagon and jumped out, striking on his feet, but whirling over and over into the ditch.

"Served him right if it broke his neck, the coward!" grated Frank.

He did not give Hodge a second glance, but, selecting a low piece of fence, he gave his entire attention to the object of reaching the road ahead of the runaway.

Toot! toot! toot! shrieked the engine of the express.

Once more the horse Frank bestrode rose handsomely to the fence. Over it he went, without touching anywhere.

Frank had seen Inza gazing at him appealingly, her face ashen with terror, and, as the horse made the leap, he shouted:

"Obey me, and I will save you!"

He could not be sure she understood, but he sincerely hoped so, for he felt that her life depended on her understanding and having nerve and strength to obey his command.

He reached the road a bit in front of the runaway, and promptly reined his horse toward the crossing. Then, looking over his shoulder, he held the animal in check sufficiently for the runaway to drag the swaying carriage alongside.

"Ready, Miss Burrage!" rang out Frank's voice, clear and strong, for all that the engine of the express seemed right upon them. "Now--rise up --jump!"

She heard him--she obeyed! His arms were outstretched, and it was not very far from the carriage to their clasp. She jumped, and fate was very kind to her just then, for she landed fairly in his clasp, and he held her there, without being unseated, a thing he could not have done had he not been a perfect horseman.

Clinging fast to his precious burden with one arm, Frank swiftly caught at the rein with his free hand. By chance more than by good judgment, he caught the proper side to draw the horse from the point of danger, and the creature bearing the double burden swept around the bend of the great U, without attempting to cross the track.

Not so the runaway. Straight upon the track plunged the mad horse. There was a crash that was heard above the sound of the wheels, which were grinding and sliding along the sanded rails, and the unfortunate runaway was hurled to its death, while the carriage was slivered to hundreds of pieces.

But Inza was saved! Saved by the brave boy she had cut and ignored a short time before.

A second time she owed her life to Frank Merriwell.

CHAPTER XXIV

HONORS FOR THE HERO

It is not strange that, after the passing of the first great wave of thankfulness, Frank Merriwell should thrill with triumph and exultation.

What a grand revenge was his! He had been humiliated that day before Bart, but he felt that he was more than even now.

He looked down at the pale face of the beautiful girl, and he saw her great dark eyes were fixed steadily on him, and in their depth was a look that bespoke unbounded thankfulness and admiration.

"You are safe, Miss Burrage," he said, when he saw that she had not fainted. "There is no longer any danger."

"The horse---"

"Was killed by the express."

She shuddered.

"And I should have been killed if I had remained in the carriage! I should have been killed but for you, for I did not have strength to jump out. I did not have strength to do anything but cling to the seat until I heard your voice, so clear and confident and commanding. That gave me strength, and I did as you wanted me to."

"Which was indeed fortunate, as I could not have saved you otherwise---I could not reach you. It was impossible to check that mad horse."

"And you did not hesitate to do all this for me

121

after---after---"

He knew what she meant, and his face hardened a bit, telling that a wound was still open in his heart.

"It was my duty. I would have tried to do as much for my worst enemy."

A shadow came to her pretty face.

"Then it was not for me in particular that you ventured so much. I had no right to expect it, but you will understand soon. I can never see that Bartley Hodge again--never! I hope he was not hurt, but, after this, I will not be forced into anything against my will."

Frank caught eagerly at her words.

"Forced?" he repeated. "What do you mean by that? Were you forced into anything? Were you compelled to accept the attentions of Hodge and cut me? It cannot be your parents---"

"My parents had nothing to do with it. You know my brother got into a bad scrape at the academy---Hodge could have caused his expulsion. Walter knew Hodge fancied me a little, and he begged me to save him. I wrote Hodge a letter, entreating him to spare my brother, and he agreed, but I was forced to make very bitter terms with him, as he demanded that I decline to see you again and cut you in public. I---I love my brother---"

Frank saw she was breaking down, and he broke in swiftly:

"Say no more, Miss Burrage; I understand it all, and I cannot blame you."

"You forgive me?"

"Yes."

"Call me Inza, please."

"Inza!"

The way he spoke the name carried the blood to her cheeks and temples, and it was by a mighty effort of will that the boy crushed back a great desire to kiss her then and there, regardless of the many eyes he knew must be watching them.

She must have read this fact in his eyes, for she half-whispered:

"I will be at home when you call next time--- Frank!"

His arms were still about her, and he held her close to his beating heart. Between them there was now a perfect understanding.

And now, suddenly returning to a full realization of their surroundings, he held her securely with one arm, while he reined the gallant horse with the other hand, whirling squarely about in the road, and returning toward the railway.

The express had come to a full stop, but, finding nothing more serious than the killing of the runaway horse and the smashing of the carriage, it was already starting onward again.

A crowd of people was swiftly collecting about the remains of the horse and carriage, and men and women were running toward the scene of the catastrophe from all directions.

It is astonishing how swiftly, even in a small country village, a crowd will collect when anything like a fire or a serious accident takes place.

Some of the people were hurrying along the road toward the boy on the horse and the rescued girl. A man in a carriage was driving toward them, and, as she saw them, Inza said:

"It is Dr. Haskell. He must have seen the accident."

This was true. Dr. Haskell drove up, crying:

"Young man, you shall have a medal of honor for saving a life! That was the bravest and noblest act I ever saw in all my life! It was astonishing--- wonderful---amazing' Give me that girl--put her right into this carriage. I will take her home! It was wonderful--astonishing--amazing!'' he repeated, with excitement and admiration.

Frank was not a little reluctant to let Inza leave his arms, but he saw that it was best, and so, riding close to the doctor's carriage, he handed her over to his ardent admirer.

As the doctor assisted her to a seat by his side, he said:

"This young gentleman saved you from being instantly killed, Miss Inza."

"And he is the one who saved me from being bitten by the mad dog," she explained.

"Is that so!" shouted the delighted and admiring doctor. "Then he ought to have two medals---by thunder, he should! An account of both deeds shall be sent to Congress, and we will see if they will not award him a medal. Yes, we will!"

Frank was blushing like a schoolgirl, and he could not say a word.

"Give me your hand, my boy!" continued the effusive physician. "I am proud to shake hands with the bravest boy I ever saw!"

Dr. Haskell nearly wrung Frank's hand off in his excitement.

The crowd was beginning to gather around them, and, feeling confused and abashed, Merriwell said:

"I think I will take this horse to the stable, doctor. Goodbye for the present, Miss Burrage."

She bade him remember his promise to call; and then he touched the horse with his whip and cantered away.

The crowd near the crossing where the accident took place saw him coming, and they stared at him until he was near at hand, and then a big man with a big voice shouted:

"Three cheers for him! Hip, hip, hurrah!"

"Hurrah! hurrah! hurrah!" roared the crowd.

Frank bowed his acknowledgment, still blushing furiously, and rode onward.

CHAPTER XXV

ON TOP

In the meantime, Bart had picked himself up from the ditch into which he had rolled after his cowardly act in leaping from the carriage and leaving his companion to her fate. Although he had received some severe bruises and abrasions, not a bone had been broken.

"Oh, Lord! what have I done?" he gasped, as he stood staring after the runaway, expecting to see Inza carried to her death. "Why didn't I grab her and take her along when I jumped!"

Then he saw Frank, saw the black horse and gallant rider sail over the fence, saw them reach the side of the carriage, and witnessed the rescue.

It is but fair to say that Bart was sincerely eager for Frank to save the girl, for he knew how much scorn and blame would fall on him if she were killed by the express, and, besides that, he was not vile enough to be unconcerned whether Inza was killed or not, so long as he was safe.

For all of the various reprehensible traits of his nature, Bart was not irredeemably bad by any means. He was passionate and vengeful, and, in times of peril, he was likely to lose his head and do the wrong thing, as he had done in this case. But, now that it was done and there was no way of undoing it, Bart would have given anything he owned had he remained in the carriage and either saved Inza or met death with her.

"What will they think of me?" he muttered, bitterly.

"What will people say? They will call me a coward, and they will pronounce Merriwell a hero! What made me jump without her! Oh, I was a fool, and I hate myself for it!"

He saw the express come to a stop, and saw the crowd collecting.

"I can never face them," he muttered, as he slipped the fence and skulked away. "I must keep out of sight."

He did not go to the livery stable where he had hired the team.

"I will just drop him a note, and say the governor'll pay for the turn-out," he decided. "Oh, but won't the old man cut up when he hears what has happened!"

And so, keeping out of sight as much as possible, he found his way back to the academy, where Frank found him in his room some time later.

Hodge expected that Merriwell would show his triumph, but, to his surprise, the boy whom the whole town of Fardale was praising as a noble hero made no outward show of exultation or triumph.

Bart thought, "He's got a queer way of rubbing it in, but it hurts just the same. I rather wish he would be a little different. He doesn't act as if he considers me worth his scorn."

But Bart was to suffer enough when the story was generally known at the academy, which happened before nightfall. He found himself scorned and held in contempt, while Merriwell was honored and regarded as a hero.

Bart's sensitive soul was almost crushed by this; but he quickly started a story that he had not jumped from the carriage, but had been thrown out by its swayings as he was rising to get a better hold on the reins. This he insisted was the truth.

126

Immediately Merriwell was questioned on this point. When asked whether Bart's statement was true, he said:

"I do not know. It may be, and I hope it is, for I do not wish to think any fellow would desert a girl under similar circumstances."

But Bart felt the disgrace so keenly that, when writing his father to send a check in payment for the destroyed team, he asked to be taken out of Fardale Academy.

In reply Mr. Hodge promptly sent the check, made out payable to the order of the proprietor of the livery stable, and assured his son that he must remain in Fardale, finishing by repeating his threat to set him adrift to "hoe his own row" in case he should be expelled.

There was nothing left but to stay, and so Hodge resolved to brace up and "face the music" as best he could. If his father was so determined to keep him at Fardale, he would make the "old man" furnish plenty of cash, and by a liberal expenditure of dollars he hoped to purchase popularity.

It had been his ambition to be among the first to be assigned to the first squad to receive uniforms, but in this he was disappointed, and he bit his tongue in anger when he heard Merriwell's name read on the list.

"That fellow is on top now," he muttered, "but there is another time coming. Things will change."

CHAPTER XXVI

FRANK RECEIVES THE MEDAL

An extraordinary scene was taking place on the parade ground of Fardale Military Academy.

I t was Saturday afternoon, and the cadets had been in camp a full week. On the plain to the west of the parade ground the white tents were pitched in four rows, making three streets within the camp. These streets were known as A, B, and C, and the tents occupied by the new scholars, or "plebes," were in the last row, facing on C street.

Just now the camp seemed entirely deserted.

There was a large number of visitors on the plain, as well as a great throng of cadets, all mingling freely and gathered around a common center, where Professor Zenas Gunn was making a speech.

Evidently the cadets had been participating in various sports, which had been interrupted by the professor, who had called them together for some purpose known to himself and a few chosen ones who were gathered around him, among whom were the assistant professors, Scotch and Jenks.

Professor Scotch's full name was Horace Orman Tyler Scotch, and, quick to seize upon anything of the sort, with the aid of the first three initials, the cadets had nicknamed him "Hot" Scotch. He was a small man, with very fiery hair and whiskers, which, together with a peppery temper, made the name seem very applicable.

Professor Jenks was more than six feet tall, and

very slim. His first name was Hyson, and so it naturally came about that he was known among the cadets as "High Jinks."

Between Professor Scotch and Professor Jenks on the platform was seated Frank Merriwell, whose face wore a flushed, bewildered, expectant expression.

Like his "plebe" companions and the members of the upper classes gathered around, he was utterly at a loss to understand what Professor Gunn was up to, and he felt his cheeks burning hotly, much to his discomfort. All he knew was that he had been captured and marched to this spit, where he was placed between the two under-professors, like a desperate criminal between officers of the law.

When the cadet band had played a lively air to draw the crowd around, Professor Gunn began his speech. All listened with curiosity expressed on their faces.

The professor was given to great verbosity, and it was some time before any one could get the drift of his remarks. He made a long preamble, having a great deal to say about the Academy and its rules, which was entirely foreign to the subject to which he was leading, or, rather, trying to approach. At length, however, he began to speak in a complimentary manner of the young gentlemen cadets, and more than one suspected he had something pleasant in store for Merriwell. Finally he described the heroism of a new member at the school, speaking in glowing terms of his noble daring in fighting the mad dog, and in saving Miss Burrage from death beneath the engine of the express.

"A full and concise account of these grand and thrilling acts of bravery, made out by Lawyer Howe, of Fardale, signed by myself and my assistants, properly witnessed and sworn to, was sent to the Congress of the United States," continued Professor

Gunn. "And now the young gentleman who thus twice saved Miss Burrage from death, and whom I am proud to own as a cadet at this academy, is about to be rewarded as he properly deserves. With no unnecessary delay, Congress ordered a medal of honor struck off for Frank Harrison Merriwell, and I have called you together for the purpose of presenting it publicly to the one for whom it was designed. Mr. Merriwell, stand up, sir!"

Frank rose to his feet, feeling that he sincerely wished himself in China, or any place but where he was at that moment. A great shout of applause went up from the crowd, and he feared the blood would come bursting through his cheeks. His head swam, and there seemed to be a haze over the faces upturned to him -- a haze that parted at one point, and showed him one face that gave him nerve and courage.

It was that of the girl he had twice saved---Inza Burrage. She was gazing at him proudly, admiringly, and she smiled her encouragement.

"My boy," said Professor Gunn, speaking as he had never before been known to address a member of the academy, with something like a touch of genuine affection, "it gives me unbound satisfaction and pleasure to be the one to present this beautiful medal. I will place it here on your chest, over a heart that is brave and noble, and may the sight of it always serve as an inspiration to you, and while it reminds you of the past, I trust it will, by reviving and keeping fresh such a memory, lead you to still grander things in the future. Again I say I am proud of you, and I am proud to number you among the young gentlemen students of this academy. I trust that your noble example will be of lasting influence and value to those with whom you are associated. That's all."

"Thank you, sir," said Frank.

Then the band struck up a lively air, the crowd cheered, and a swarm of Frank's admirers lifted him on their shoulders and carried him away.

CHAPTER XXVII

AMBUSHED AND ROBBED

"Did you ever hear such rot as Old Gunn's spouting!" exclaimed Leslie Gage, one of the old students at the academy. "All this fuss over a plebe who has happened to do a little something that anyone else might have done in his place, makes me sick!"

"What about Hodge?" smiled Cadet Lieutenant Swift, who happened to be with Gage. "He failed to improve his opportunity."

"Hodge was unlucky," said Gage. "He says he was thrown from the rocking carriage while trying to stop the runaway horse, and I believe he tells the truth. He is a generous fellow---spends money like water."

"And I fancy his generosity has a great deal to do with your opinion as to the truth of his statement," declared Swift.

"I hope you do not mean that you think I could be bought?"

"Oh, no, I don't mean a thing---not a thing."

But the way Swift spoke the words made it all the more apparent that he did mean something, and sarcasm was evident in his face, as well as his voice.

"There's Hodge now," said Gage, as the dark-haired plebe and his friend Bascomb passed by, talking earnestly in low tones. "I want a word with him."

He hurried away after the two.

Watching, Swift saw them draw aside from the throng, and talk earnestly, with their heads close together.

"I believe they are up to no good," he muttered. "Hodge is revengeful, Bascomb is a bully, and Gage is envious of Merriwell. There is something being hatched up, and Merriwell had better watch out."

He decided to speak to the boy who had been honored in such a remarkable manner that day, and so he set out to find Frank, who had been carried away on the shoulders of his admiring friends.

It was nearly thirty minutes later when he saw Merriwell walking along one of the tree-lined avenues of the grounds with Inza Burrage by his side.

Swift hesitated, then decided to speak to Frank later, and the two passed on, happy in each other's company, the medal of honor shining on the boy's chest.

That evening Frank Merriwell walked through the twilight to Fardale village with Inza. It had been a happy day for both of them.

It had grown quite dark when Frank turned back toward the academy, and he swung along at a good pace, whistling a merry tune, his heart light and carefree.

He had no warning when, all of a sudden, dark forms darted out of the bushes by the roadside and surrounded him. He was clutched by strong hands, and a handkerchief, saturated with chloroform, was pressed over his mouth and nose.

By a desperate effort, he freed his mouth and gave a shout.

"Help!"

The shout was answered, and the sound of feet

running swiftly along the road was heard.

Exclamations of dismay and anger broke from Frank's assailants.

"We'll have to skip, fellows!" hissed one.

"Let's get out of here!" said another.

Then Frank was hurled heavily to the ground, and the dark figures melted away into the bushes.

A solitary individual came dashing up the road to the spot, as Frank sat up in a dazed way, rubbing his head, and staring around in the darkness.

"What's the matter wid ya?" asked the newcomer.

Frank recognized the voice.

"Hello, Barney!" he exclaimed. "It was lucky you were near enough to hear me when I shouted."

"By me soul!" cried Barney Mulloy; "it's Frankie, boy! What's the meaning of this?"

"It means I was waylaid---mugged---assaulted! There were five or six of them, and they had cloths or handkerchiefs tied over their faces. They jumped out of the bushes here, as I was passing."

"Ya don't mean it!"

"They froze to me," continued Frank--"tried to chloroform me! Here! here is the very handkerchief they tried to do the job with! Have a whiff of that."

Barney took it and smelled it.

"Phew!" he puffed. "It smells like it were spoiled."

"There's something behind this business," declared Frank, as he got upon his feet, assisted by the Irish lad. "I don't understand what those fellows were up to. How did you happen to be along here anyway, Barney?"

"It was Lieutenant Swift that told me ya might get in trouble, and so I came out to meet ya."

"Lieutenant Swift told you that?"

"Yeah."

"What made him tell you anything of the kind?"

"Begorra! I don't know, at all. He said he didn't have a chance to speak to ya, an' he advised me to tell ya to look out mighty sharp for yaself."

"Then he must have known something was going to happen; but I don't know why he should have sent me warning, for he is very reserved, and he will have very little to do with plebes. He has never seemed friendly toward me."

"I don't know about that; but what he said made me feel uneasy, an' so I came out to meet ya on ya way back to camp."

"I am very glad you did, Barney. Let me have that handkerchief. It may serve me a turn."

"If ya can find out who owns th' rag, ya can make it mighty warm for th' louse."

"That's right," nodded Frank. "But I would give more to know just why I was attacked in such a manner. There is a mystery about it that I do not understand."

"No more do I."

Frank took the chloroform-saturated handkerchief and placed it in his pocket. He was still a trifle giddy, and his legs felt strangely weak, but the fresh air was swiftly relieving him, and he soon became able to walk along briskly at Barney's side.

In a short time they came out where they could look down upon the cadet encampment, with the lights showing through the white tents, and the sentries pacing up and down on their beats, being plainly revealed now and then, as they passed some illuminated tent that was thrown open at both ends.

It was a pleasant spectacle, and the two boys paused to view it admiringly.

"If it weren't for the studyin', I'd like to go to school for the rest of me life," said Barney.

"You would get tired of it in time," asserted

Frank. "As for me, if it wasn't for the study-ing, I wouldn't go to school at all. I want to travel all over the world, and I mean to do so some day."

They went down and entered the grounds, pass-ing the first sentry. When the camp was reached, they were brought to a halt by sentry number two, but they gave the countersign without hesitation, and were permitted to pass on.

It was a warm evening, and the cadets were keeping to the open air. Merriwell was greeted from all sides, but he declined to join any of the groups, going straight to his tent, where he found Bart Hodge and Hans Dunnerwust. Hodge regarded Frank closely as he entered, but said nothing.

Not so Hans.

"How are you?" saluted the roly-poly Dutch boy. "You been out to take a valk mit your girl already yet, I bet your life. Yaw! Say, dat girl vas a beaut. If I don't been engaged mit Katrina since I vas five years old, I vould valk in and cut you out mit dat girl. But I don't vant to get Katrina in my hair. She is fifteen years old and veighs a hundred and seventy-five pounds. Guten Himmel! dat girl has a muscle bigger than mein head. You bet me my boots she vouldn't do a thing to me if she vas caught me valking up to some other girl!"

Hans winked with the whole side of his face as he made this final remark.

"Go on wid ya. Dutch!" cut in Barney. "Ya talk too much wid ya mouth, that's what ya do."

"Hey!" cried Hans, instantly assuming a bell-igerent mood. "Vat vas dat? If I don't learn to talk da United States better as you did, I bet me your shirt I wouldn't open mein yap! You talk same as you had your mouth full of bog-vater!"

"An' ya talk like ya had ya mouth full of sauer-kraut, Dutch."

"Don't you be callin' me Dootch, Irish!"

"I'll break ya eye if ya call me Irish!"

There seemed danger of a scrap then and there, but Frank intervened, ordering them both to keep still, and, after some grumbling, they subsided.

But Hans could not keep still long, and he soon broke out:

"You vas a lucky chap, Frankie, when you got dat medal mit da United States of Congress buy. Vat you done wid it? I vant to look at it, if you don't have no objection."

Frank glanced down at his chest where the medal had been pinned, and then he staggered back, gasping:

"It's gone!"

"Gone!" gasped Barney.

"Yes," said Frank, hoarsely; "it is gone, and I believe I've been robbed!"

CHAPTER XXVIII

THE TELLTALE HANDKERCHIEF

"Robbed?"

"Yes!"

"Guten Himmel!" gurgled Hans.

Bart Hodge said not a word, but there was a strange look on his face.

"Perhaps ya've not been robbed, Merriwell, me boy," said Barney, with an effort to reassure his friend.

"Then what has become of the medal?"

"Perhaps it was lost in the scuffle."

"That is true," came eagerly from Frank. "It may have been torn from my chest accidentally. I must go back and see. There is plenty of time before taps."

"An' I'll go wid ya."

"Me, too, by jiminy!"

"We will take a candle and some matches," said Frank, who was greatly excited and distressed. "If it is anywhere near the spot where those fellows jumped on me, we can find it."

In a very few moments they had started, and as they left the tent Bart smiled grimly, whispering to himself:

"Search as much as you like, Frank Merriwell; but I don't believe you will find your medal this night."

The trio had no trouble in getting out of the camp and beyond the grounds, although Frank did not care to let it become known he had lost the precious medal presented to him that day. He felt that such an announcement would be most disgraceful.

What would be thought of a boy careless enough to lose such a precious souvenir within a few hours after he had received it? Would he not be regarded with scorn and contempt?

His face burned, and his heart was throbbing with pent-up shame and rage. Over and over he declared to himself that, if he had been robbed, his assailants should be brought to book and made to suffer for their dastardly act.

Frank led the way up the road toward Fardale village, with Barney close at his heels, and Hans puffing along behind. They soon reached the locality where the mysterious assault had taken place.

"Now to find the exact spot where they jumped on me," said Frank, as he and Barney began looking about.

Hans asked twenty questions between his panting breaths, and Frank told him enough to keep him still.

The spot was soon found. Frank's hands shook as he tried to light the candle, and he dropped two matches and burned his fingers with the third before he succeeded.

He was hoping against hope that the precious medal would be found somewhere on the ground near that spot.

Breathlessly the three boys began the search, and they kept it up until all were satisfied that it was a vain quest.

"It is not here!" said Frank, hoarsely.

The candle trembled in his hand, and his face showed ghastly pale by the quivering, flaring light.

"That's a fact," admitted Barney, with great reluctance. "If it were here, we'd find it easy."

"There is no doubt, now, I was robbed!"

"I think ya right, me boy."

"That was the main object of the assault upon me, and the sneaking gang succeeded!"

"Yes, me boy."

"But they shall be made to suffer for it!" cried Frank, rising to his feet and holding one clenched hand above his head, while the light of the candle flared over three faces.

"If such a thing is possible, I will find out who did this dirty trick, and then---"

He stopped there, but the blank was more expressive than words could have been.

"You vant to give dat fella der rink of der blinkety-blink, as those cadets say ven they vas goin' to haze someone," put in Hans. "Ans you vas the boy to do it."

Frank was reluctant to give up the search, and he got down on his knees again, going carefully over the ground, but with the same result.

A short time later the trio returned to the camp.

Bart was still in the tent. He gave Merriwell a quick glance, and then kept his eyes turned away.

Frank knew Hodge was still his enemy, for all that they were tent-mates, and something about the fellow's manner made him suspicious. He watched Bart a moment in silence, and then he sat down to think it over. Of course he must report the loss of the medal, but he wanted a few moments to get his nerves steady.

Hans could not be kept still.

"If you don't lick the stuffin' of dat fella out when you find him, I voud do dat meinself," he declared. "He vas a sneak, dat's vat's der matter mit Hannah!"

All of a sudden, to Frank's surprise, Bart turned swiftly on him, saying:

"You didn't find the medal, did you, Merriwell?"

"No."

"You may be able to find it in the morning."

"If I do, I think I shall find it in the possession of an enemy."

"You believe you were robbed?"

"I do."

"What are you going to do about it?"

"Report it to Lieutenant Gordan and Professor Gunn."

Now it happened that Lieutenant Gordan was passing the tent at this moment, and he heard Merriwell's words. Into the tent he stepped, saying:

"I am here, Mr. Merriwell, if you have anything to report."

In a moment the four boys sprang up, saluted, and stood at attention.

Frank hesitated, his face getting crimson again. It was a bitter pill to swallow, but he must confess that he had lost the medal, and so, after some stammering, he related his story.

The lieutenant listened silently, his face growing hard and stern. When Frank had finished, he asked:

"Have you any reason to suspect your assailants were cadets of Fardale Academy, Mr. Merriwell?"

"I suspect they were, for I know of no reason why anyone else should waylay and rob me."

"But do you know of any reason why your fellow-students should commit such a reprehensible act?"

"No sir; no good reason."

"Have you enemies among them?"

"I think so, sir."

"More than one?"

"Not more than one that I know as an enemy, sir."

Bart Hodge's face had paled a bit, but now it grew dark with anger, and he flashed Merriwell a fierce look.

"Then you have one whom you know as an enemy?"

"Yes, sir; he has shown himself my enemy in the past."

"Will you name him?"

"I beg you to excuse me, sir; I cannot."

"But it may aid a great deal in the recovery of your medal."

"It might, sir; and it might bring suspicion on one who is entirely innocent. I cannot name him, sir."

Bart's face cleared, and, for the first time in his life, he felt like shaking Frank's hand.

Lieutenant Gordan did not show approval, but, to tell the truth, he had not expected Merriwell would name anyone as a known enemy.

"Very well," he said, "I will report the matter to Professor Gunn, and we will see what can be done. If we find out the guilty party or parties belong to this school, I promise you they shall be expelled. I don't suppose you have any clue to the perpetrators of the outrage."

"I have this, sir," said Frank, taking the chloroformed handkerchief from his pocket and passing it to the officer, who unfolded it for inspection.

A gasp of dismay came from Bart Hodge's lips, and his face grew ashen.

CHAPTER XXIX

"TOBOGGANED"

That gasp was enough to attract Lieutenant Gordan's attention, and he glanced quickly and keenly at Hodge.

Bart caught his breath again, and---sneezed!

It was done skillfully and naturally, so it seemed that the first gasp was but a forerunner of the sneeze.

He immediately begged pardon.

"I trust you have not taken cold, Mr. Hodge," said the lieutenant, in a queer way.

Thank you, sir; I think not,"said Bart.

Lieutenant Gordan continued the inspection of the handkerchief.

"Here is a letter in the corner---an 'H.' If it were a monogram it might lead immediately to the discovery o f the owner and the culprit; but this letter was plainly made in the handkerchief. However, it is a most important clue, and it will go hard with the fellow who has other handkerchiefs like this."

He carefully folded the handkerchief and put it into his pocket.

Bart looked as if he longed to snatch it, but he made no move.

After assuring Frank that everything possible to discover the guilty ones would be done, the lieutenant left the tent.

"There's plenty of fellas that have names beginnin' with H," said the Irish lad. "There's Harris, Hardy, Higgins, Hodge---"

He stopped short and stared at Bart, his mouth open.

"Well," snapped the dark-haired youth, "what are you stopping there for? Go on and name the others."

"I didn't know but I had named enough," said Barney, in an insinuating tone.

Bart clenched his hands and seemed on the point of making a rush at the Irish lad; but, if he had such intentions, he suddenly changed his mind.

"Just what do you mean by that?" he asked, controlling his voice remarkably.

"Mean? Why, I named four, an' I didn't know but that were enough."

"Oh, you are very sharp."

"Don't mention it. There do be sharper ones than meself behind iron bars, to say nothing of you, me boy."

Frank was saying nothing, but not a word did he miss. He did not wish to think Hodge had been one of his assailants, but his old enemy was certainly acting in a manner calculated to arouse suspicion. Then the handkerchief with an "H" in one corner was quite enough to make him believe it possible Hodge had taken a hand in the affair.

If so, and it was proved against him, it meant expulsion for Hodge.

Frank had not intended that the loss of his medal should become generally known right away, but the story got out some way, and, before taps, several parties came to the tent to express sympathy, or to ask questions. They were received pleasantly, but it became apparent that Merriwell did not wish to talk.

The news spread, and before the signal for retiring sounded the entire camp knew what had happened. That matter was discussed in A, B, and C streets, and, while some were inclined to smile over the plebe's misfortune, all agreed that it would go hard with the guilty parties if they were found out.

Somehow, the presentation of that medal had seemed to arouse a strong feeling of jealousy among the cadets. Before that occurred, Frank had seemed like a general favorite, but there were now many who seemed to covertly rejoice at his loss.

"The plebe won't swell around with that thing dangling before our eyes holidays," said one. "Why he would have had the swelled head so bad that his superiors would not have been good enough for him to speak to outside the grounds."

"I think you misjudge Frank Merriwell," said another. "I do not believe he is the kind of a fellow to swell around. I think Merriwell is a fine fellow."

"Think what you like," came sharply from the first. "I shan't cry over the loss of his medal."

"There are lots with you," said another envious fellow. "For myself, I think that particular plebe has fared altogether too easily since coming here. He has scarcely been run through the mill at all."

"That's so," joined in a third. "He has had a soft time of it; but I'm in for making up for lost time."

"What do you mean?"

"It's going to be a fine night for tobogganing."

The cadets seemed to understand this, for they smiled, and one observed:

"It will be darker than a pocket."

"Let's give him a slide."

"That goes."

"What time?"

"About eleven."

"We will be there."

Tattoo gave them warning, and the sounding of taps found every tent dark and silent. The sentries

144

paced their beats, and began calling the hours promptly at the proper time.

"Eleven o'clock, and a-l-l-'-s well," passed around the slumbering camp, and the eyes of the sentries saw nothing to arouse their suspicions, their ears heard no sound to tell them that a night raid on plebes was about to be made.

Frank had remained awake, for all that it was necessary for him to be in bed at the regular hour. He could not sleep. The misfortune that had come upon him was so crushing that his spirit writhed in anguish, and it was with difficulty that he kept from making some unnecessary noise, which would have earned him a rebuke and demerit.

He heard the sentries call the hour of eleven, but it was as if they were far away---many miles distant. He was in a sort of stupor. Barney was breathing regularly at his side, and the breathing from the other bed revealed that Bart and Hans were fast asleep.

It might have been ten minutes past eleven when he thought he heard someone stirring outside the tent. Still he remained in a sort of stupor, idly wondering what it could mean. Had he heard anything, or was it imagination?

Another five minutes slipped away, and then---

Merriwell never knew exactly how it happened, but he felt himself jerked out of bed, rolled in his blanket, and, thus enveloped, dragged by the heels about the camp. In language of the academy, he was given a "toboggan slide."

At the same time, Barney, Bart, and Hans had been yanked out of bed in the same mysterious manner.

"It's the old boy himself!" groaned the Irish lad, as he felt his feet grasped by the mysterious power and found himself swiftly sliding across the floor of the tent. "I'm done for entirely!"

"Guten Himmel!" cried the Dutch lad. "Vat vas der matter mit me? Vas I shackled onto some express train already yet? Wow! Broke avay mit dat feet if you don't vant to get a corner of your jaw kicked off!"

Then the blanket covered his head and smothered his voice, and he found himself taking a "toboggan slide."

The sound of this racket was heard by the nearest sentry, who challenged, and then shouted:

"Corporal of the guard! Corporal of the guard!"

That cry was enough to bring the corporal down from the guard tents at a run. The officer of the guard also hurried to the point from which the alarm came, but when the reached that spot he found a deserted tent, the bedding being scattered and the plebes gone. The sentry could tell them nothing save that he had heard smothered cries and running feet.

Then came the search for the captured plebes, who were finally found at the farther extremity of the camp, having just crawled from their dust-covered blankets, stunned, dazed, and unable to speak coherently.

Barney was so mad that he could do nothing but claw the air and gasp, while Hans was half-laughing and half-crying, as he muttered:

"If I find meinself in less than twenty-seven pieces, I bet me your life I don't been afraid of cyclones and earthquakes after dat!"

CHAPTER XXX

A LIVELY NIGHT

When questioned, Bart Hodge said he didn't know who his assailants were, but he was fierce in his denunciation of the "outrage," until sternly silenced by the officer of the guard.

The corporal of the guard was trying to get something out of Frank Merriwell, but Frank had little to say, save that he had not the least idea in the world who had dragged him around the camp in his blanket. He seemed to regard it as a good joke, and did not utter a word for which he could be rebuked, much to the corporal's disgust.

Lieutenant Gordan had heard the outcry, and he came down with a bull's-eye lantern, by the light of which he looked the four plebes over.

Hodge was wiping the dust and a little blood from his cheek with a corner of the blanket, and tried to express himself to the lieutenant, only to be cut off and again silenced in a way that was most annoying to him.

"Make an immediate inspection, Mr. Harris," directed Lieutenant Gordan, speaking to the officer of the guard. "Mr. Otis and I will attend to these young gentlemen. Take this lantern, sir."

So Mr. Harris took the lantern and went about inspection, while the lieutenant and Otis conducted the four plebes back to their tent.

It must be said to Mr. Harris' credit that he made the inspection faithfully, but he knew plenty of time had been given for the hazers to get back to their beds, and he was not surprised to find the cadets sleeping soundly, to all outward appearance, for all of the disturbance in camp.

The four "tobogganed" plebes were escorted back to their tent, where they were allowed to light one candle while their beds were hastily made beneath the eye of Lieutenant Gordan, and they turned in again.

Hodge paused long enough to get a handkerchief to wipe the blood from his cheek.

By the light of the candle, Frank saw something on the corner of that handkerchief---something that made his eyes blaze. He made a move to snatch the handkerchief, but seemed to change his mind suddenly, and, for the time, Bart escaped being denounced.

The first night in camp at Fardale had always been a tumultuous one for plebes, but it had started differently this year, much to the satisfaction of Professor Gunn and Lieutenant Gordan, who began to flatter themselves that better discipline had been established, and that really there was little or no hazing at the academy.

Lieutenant Gordan had actually been an officer in the regular army at one time, and he was a graduate of West Point. Why he was not still in the army was not exactly clear, for it could not be discovered that he had left anything but a most honorable record behind him, having seen actual service in a campaign, at which time his superior had spoken of him as a brave and efficient officer.

The lieutenant aspired to model the school at Fardale so much on the lines followed at West Point that it would be regarded by military people, as well as by regular citizens, as the leading private school of that character in the country.

Hazing in camp had been found even more difficult to prevent than hazing in barracks. At West Point rows of gas lamps stand along the sentry lines, and these, with other precautions, made it a very hazardous thing for the old cadets to attempt to "devil" plebes.

There were no gas lamps at Fardale. The camp was wrapped in darkness, save for the light of the moon and stars, which was not always regular, and could never be regarded as sufficient.

Sentries had been kidnapped while on duty, and all manner of pranks had been played at Fardale. Professor Gunn's remonstrances and Lieutenant Gordan's threats had been equally insufficient to put a check to this; but, for some reason, this particular year had seen very few of these things happen.

When the "tobogganed" plebes were securely in bed again, the lieutenant made the rounds of the sentries, testing their knowledge of their duties, and warning them to be fully and constantly on the alert. He did not trust this matter wholly to the corporal of the relief, whose duty it was to see that every sentry was at his post and answered promptly and correctly the catechism.

By the time he had made the rounds, "Twelve o'clock, and a-l-l-'-s well," ran around the camp.

It was Sunday morning, and the lieutenant did not suppose there would be any further disturbance, so he retired again, hoping to sleep soundly until reveille.

But the excitement for the night was not yet over. There was no intention of letting the "tobogganed" plebes sleep quietly until morning.

 And so it came about that Bart Hodge was just beginning to dream that he was battling over a handkerchief with Merriwell, and Merriwell was an elephant that had crushed him to the ground and was smothering him, when he awoke to find himself enveloped in the tent, which had come tumbling down upon them all.

It was exceedingly dark, and, wondering what had happened, Bart managed to get out of bed, when he felt himself clutched once more, and, before he could make an outcry, tumbled into a rickety wheelbarrow, which was surrounded by a score of dark figures. Then away they went, bumping, swaying, creaking, and rattling around the camp, Bart's teeth chattering with the jolts, and a sort of stuttering howl of rage coming from his lips.

Hans Dunnerwust tried to keep still and escape, but this did not work. He was yanked out into the open air, and, before he could say "Guten Himmel" more than once, he was perched astride the tentpole , which lay along several strong shoulders.

"Let 'er rip!" said a low voice.

On either side there were hands to keep the Dutch lad upright on the pole, to which he clung frantically. They started at a run with him, and he let out a wild howl of terror and distress.

"Help! Help!" cried the Dutch boy. "If I don't been killed der other time, am I now? I have ridden mit an express train on, and straddled a jackmule, but dat isn't as bad as dis kind of a beast! Help!" he squawked, as he tried to tie his fat legs in a square knot on the under side of the pole. "If somebody don't help me down from dis beast, I bet me mein life I vas dead already yet right away! If I ever live until morning, I am going to take out ten thousand dollar insurance on mein life, you betcha, den, ven I vas killed, I been paid for it enough to make me reach der rest of mein life. Help! Help! If I don't get down off dat pole, I been cut in two already yet, and I find meinself twins der morning in."

And so his wild cries trailed all the way around the camp.

150

All of a sudden, he was dropped heavily to the ground, where he sat rubbing his eyes and staring into the darkness, for everyone of the dark forms had vanished like magic, and he was quite alone.

"If I don't feel dat place vere I vas cut in two, I bet me more than zwi dollars I have took a ride on der nightmare. I have heard of dat kind of a horse before, and I think I have been out for a little turn mit him dis evening. Yaw! Dat vas the matter mit Hannah!"

In the meantime, Merriwell and Mulloy had been rolled into the center of the tent-fly, and then they were tossed, kicking and struggling, into the air, to fall on the fly and be tossed again, by the grim band that surrounded it and held it stretched clear of the ground.

"Begorra!" gasped Barney; "it's a lovely kind of a night this do be, I dunno!"

"Rather so," admitted Frank, coolly.

"Wow!" howled the Irish lad, as they bounced into the air, clutching wildy at each other. "This beats life on the bounding billow, Merriwell, me boy!"

But soon the bouncing became so lively that they could not exchange a word, and it was kept up for some minutes.

All at once a voice said:

"Next time--drop!"

Down they came, and they found themselves in the midst of their demolished tent, while the dark figures had vanished.

The alarm had been given, and the sentry came panting to the spot. The corporal of the guard quickly appeared, and Lieutenant Gordon, now thoroughly aroused, was not far behind him.

"I will make an immediate inspection of the tents, Mr. Otis," said the lieutenant. "Someone should be punished for this piece of work! See that the tent is put up as soon as possible. Take the name of the sentry on this post. This matter shall be sifted."

Then he hurried away.

But Lieutenant Gordon's inspection proved no more effective than had Harris' less than two hours before. Everything seemed all right everywhere except at that one particular collapsed tent.

"It's little sleep we'll get tonight," thought Frank, as he assisted in the reconstruction of the tent. "We are marked for trouble, and we are getting it."

Hodge and Hans were found and brought back, both seeming badly broken up by what they had been through.

The tent was set up in a remarkably brief space of time, and then the four plebes turned in once more.

Lieutenant Gordon saw that extra sentries were posted at that side of the camp, all of whom were directed to give special attention to the tent that seemed to contain the objects singled out for "torture" by the mischievous cadets.

Then followed a long lull, and it seemed that the excitement was over for the night.

But it was not.

Tired and sore, the four occupants of the tent fell asleep. Morning was not far away, but it was still very dark when---

"Atchew!"

A smothered sneeze came from Barney.

There were a few moments of silence, and then, from the other bed, came a more violent sneeze:

"A-a-a-atchew!"

It sounded like Hans.

Frank awoke and caught his breath.

"Atchew!" he sneezed.

"Atchew! atchew! a-a-atchew!" burst from Barney.

"By me soul, it's the top of me head I split that time!" muttered the Irish lad, sleepily. "I must have a bad cold in me head, I dunno."

"Atchew!" sneezed Hodge, who was not awake.

"Atchew! atchew! atchew!" roared Hans, the last sneeze nearly throwing him out of the bed. "Guten Himmel! Vat vas der matter mit mein nose?"

And then they went at it all together:

"Atchew! Atchew! Atchew!"

Holy smoke!" gurgled Barney. "I feel like I had a whole swarm of flies crawling up my nose, an'every fly had a hundred an'seventeen feet to crawl with!"

"Say!" gasped Hans; "if I don't have der hose turned up mein nose pretty soon already, I vas going to sneeze der roof of mein head off!"

"What is the matter?" asked Frank, speaking for the first time. "I believe I smell smoke!"

Clinging to his nose, he quickly got out of bed and opened the fly of the tent to admit fresh air.

At this moment the sentry demanded to know the cause of the commotion in there.

Frank explained that the tent was full of smoke.

And then he found an old iron kettle, in which some kind of a substance was slowly burning, sending up a volume of smoke. Remembering his early school days, Frank knew red pepper had been sprinkled plentifully on the burning substance, and it was this that had caused the sneezing.

It was now so near morning that no further pranks could be perpetrated, but it had been a very lively night, to say the least.

CHAPTER XXXI

A CASE OF NERVE

For all that the following day was Sunday, the boys were not only forced to spend a great deal of time in getting their tent into order, but were also required to attend services in the chapel and be prompt as usual in their other duties.

The interruptions and excitement of the night did not absolve either Hodge or Dunnerwust from a sharp reproof at morning inspection, when they appeared in ranks looking negligent and careless as to dress. Hans said not a word, having already learned to keep silent under such circumstances, and did not even grin; but Hodge was in bad humor, and he muttered behind the officer's back.

This was promptly and sharply checked, and the demerit recorded, "Hodge, belt and pompom awry, muttering in ranks."

It is not strange that the four boys were rather listless and dispirited, and it was with the greatest difficulty Hans succeeded in keeping awake during the morning service.

There was more or less bantering when the battalion assembled for breakfast, and this was renewed at dinner.

"Mr. Merriwell," said one smiling cadet, "they tell me you are a great traveler, and that you are particularly fond of coasting. Now, would you mind stating just what sort of coasting you prefer? Is tobogganing in your line?"

"I have found tobogganing very lively and diverting, sir," replied Frank, respectfully, a sly twinkle in his eye.

"And you, Mr. Hodge---what do you think of it?"

"I think it is an outrage that such things can be carried on in a school that is supposed to be for young gentlemen!" was the hot reply.

"Mr. Bond," said the smiling cadet, suddenly growing sober, and turning sharply to a comrade, "will you be good enough to record Mr. Hodge's words. Be careful to take them down exactly as they were spoken---'a school that is supposed to be for young gentlemen.'"

Mr. Bond immediately and gravely made a show of taking down the speech, much to Bart's dismay and uneasiness.

"Now, Mr. Mulloy," said the questioner, whose name was Hawkins, "it is reported that you are a great aeronaut---that you have even been known to make ascensions in the night. I would like to know what you think of the business of aerial navigation."

"Well," said Barney, in his most whimsical way, "I find there to be a great many ups and downs to it."

This sent a smile over the assembly, and Hawkins turned next to Hans, who was looking sleepy and dull.

"They tell me you have also traveled, Mr. Dunnerwust," said the teasing cadet. "Which method of travel do you prefer?"

"Vell," replied the Dutch boy, promptly, "I don't been stuck on dat traveling by rail."

And the whole table roared with delight.

That afternoon was spent in studying and writing letters. Frank had several to write, and he found an opportunity to do so without interruption.

He had finished his last letter and stepped to the front of the tent, when he saw Hodge, Leslie Gage, and Cadet Hawkins talking earnestly together some distance down the street. Gage immediately saw Frank appear, and, with a low word to the

155

others, he walked away.

It seemed, however, that Hodge and Hawkins were engaged in some angry altercation, and they did not mind that Merriwell was watching them.

All at once, to Frank's amazement, Bart suddenly and swiftly slapped Hawkins across the face with a glove, which he held in his hand. Hawkins would have returned the blow with one straight from the shoulder, but Hodge leaped back, and twenty cadets, who had been watching the two from a distance, rushed in and dragged the two apart, hustling them away so the officers should see nothing they would be forced to report.

Frank muttered, "That means a fight, and Hodge deliberately brought it on! I wonder what it is about?"

A short time later Bart came to the tent, his face still flushed. To Frank's surprise, he spoke:

"Did you see me slap that fellow, Merriwell?" he asked.

"Yes."

"Well, he insulted me---he charged me with being concerned in the stealing of your medal."

"Well, weren't you?" asked Frank, coolly.

Bart dropped back a step, and then promptly answered:

"No, sir; I had nothing whatever to do with it."

"How about that handkerchief with your intitial in the corner."

"I knew you would bring that up. It is something that puzzles me."

"Then you acknowledge that the handkerchief was yours?"

"No. It certainly was like mine; but I do not believe it was mine."

"You do not believe it? What do you know about it?"

"I know it was not mine, unless it was stolen

156

from me."

A cold smile came to Frank's face.

"Doesn't that strike you as a little thin, Hodge? Do you expect to squirm out of it that way?"

Hodge flung out one hand, with a desperate gesture.

"You have every reason to be down on me, Merriwell," he confessed. "I acknowledge that; but I swear to you that I had no hand in the stealing of your medal."

"The handkerchief, which is in Lieutenant Gordan's possession, will prove a strong piece of evidence against you, I reckon."

"It may serve to make some trouble for me, but, as evidence, it will amount to nothing."

"How is that?"

"I shall prove an alibi."

"An alibi?"

"Yes, sir."

"How?"

"I can prove that I did not leave the limits of the camp on the night that you were waylaid and robbed---last night."

"You say you can prove this?"

"I do. If I prove it, I have a favor to ask of you."

"What favor?"

"I want you to be my second in the fight with Hawkins."

Frank was fairly staggered by the nerve of this request.

"Don't you think you are asking rather too much of me, Hodge?" he said, slowly. "We have never been friends, and your fight with Hawkins came about, as you have said, through his charging you with having a hand in the robbery of the medal. I should think you could see that, under the circumstances, I am in a position where I cannot act as your second."

"Then you refuse?" asked Bart, bitterly.

"I am obliged to."

"Oh, all right! It is the first time I have seen fit to ask a favor of you, and it will be the last! I am willing to bury the hatchet and be friendly, but I see you will not have it so. I have told you the truth about having had nothing to do with the stealing of your medal, as I shall prove to your satisfaction---or dissatisfaction. You hate me, and I suppose you would be glad to see me expelled from the academy."

"I have no love for you, Hodge," said the other lad, frankly; "but I have no desire to injure you as long as you do right and let me alone. You should know this by the past, for I could have kept you out of the academy had I seen fit to tell the truth concerning you."

"So you fling that in my face! All right! all right! You may think you are too good to have anything to do with me; but I assure you that my people move in circles that neither you nor any of your relations could ever enter. I shall have nothing to do with you in the future---"

"Which will be a great relief to me."

Hodge bit his lip, restraining a violent outburst of anger with no little difficulty.

Somehow he had formed the idea that, for all of the past, Merriwell would be only too glad to accept him as a friend, and it galled his proud spirit to have his overtures rebuffed.

As for Frank, it seemed possible that Hodge realized the handkerchief had placed him in a very bad fix, and he had made this desperate "bluff" in order to make it seem that Merriwell was his friend and did not think him concerned in the robbery, for it would certainly have seemed that way had Frank consented to act as his second.

But the game did not work, and Hodge departed

in a huff, after again declaring he would prove an alibi as far as the robbery was concerned.

CHAPTER XXXII

ESTABLISHING AN ALIBI

Bart seemed to be in earnest, for he went directly to Professor Gunn, whom he told how the handkerchief bearing his initial had been used in the assault upon Merriwell, and how it had been delivered to Lieutenant Gordan, who was about to call a court of inquiry.

"Well, well, well!" exclaimed the professor. "And you say the handkerchief is yours?"

"No, sir. What I say is that it is exactly like mine."

"And you deny that you had any hand in the attack upon and robbery of Mr. Merriwell?"

"Most emphatically, sir."

"But how do you explain this handkerchief business?"

"I do not attempt to explain it further than to say that, if the handkerchief is mine, it must have been stolen from the laundry, or given some other fellow by mistake."

"Slim, sir---slim! It looks bad. If you are really innocent, this handkerchief affair is most unfortunate for you."

"But I want you to call an investigation before Lieutenant Gordan proceeds to that extreme. I will prove to your satisfaction that I did not leave the limits of the camp that evening. That ought to settle this matter so far as I am concerned."

The professor finally agreed to call a meeting

and give Bart an opportunity to prove his claim. Bart gave the names of those he wished to be present, and then departed, muttering:

"I will clear myself of this scrape, and then I will do my best to lick Hawkins. If I succeed, it will come pretty near setting me right with the fellows who are down on me. And I ought to give Hawkins a tight go, for, ever since my fight with Frank Merriwell, I have been taking boxing lessons, with the idea of getting at Merriwell again and doing him in."

Had it not been Sunday, without doubt Hodge would have been waited on immediately by a friend of Hawkins. At Fardale, however, it was a point of honor never to fight on Sundays, nor to transact any business in connection with a fight, so nothing further was done that day, although it had become plain that something unusual was taking place, for there was an air of suppressed excitement all over the camp.

Lieutenant Gordan had been at work, and Hodge would have been called to explain the handkerchief matter by him had not Professor Gunn requested him to delay this questioning a short time.

The lieutenant did not know why the professor made such a request, but, although he was not quite pleased by it, he agreed.

During the forenoon of the next day no time was given for Hawkins to send a friend to confer with Hodge's second, and so it came about that before going into the fight, Bart was given an opportunity to prove his innocence in regard to the assault and robbery.

Frank Merriwell was notified to appear at a certain hour in one of the academy rooms, and when he arrived there, he found quite a little company assembled.

The three professors were there, looking solemn

and dignified. Lieutenant Gordan was on hand, seeming rather displeased, as if he did not relish having a matter in his province interfered with; Cadet Lieutenant Swift, Cadet Corporal Burrage, and plebes Gray and Davis were also present, wearing puzzled expressions on their faces, as if they did not understand just what it was all about, and Bartley Hodge was on hand, looking cool and confident, as if there was no reason on earth why he should be anxious.

As soon as Merriwell appeared, the doors were locked, and Professor Gunn made known the reason why they were assembled there.

As usual, he was very verbose, having a great deal to say that might well have been omitted, but he finally made it hazily plain that they had come together at Hodge's request to give him a chance to prove his innocence in connection with the assault and robbery of Merriwell. An object of the secret investigation and hearing was to prevent any false moves, as it certainly would have been a false move had Hodge been arraigned and charged with something of which he was entirely innocent, as he could readily prove.

Lieutenant Gordan smiled sarcastically, but said nothing. He declined to press any charge against Hodge, saying that such an investigation was unmilitary and entirely out of his line.

Then it fell on Professor Gunn to make further explanation, which he did, exhibiting the marked handkerchief that had been saturated with chloroform and used to overcome Merriwell, and showing one of Hodge's, which was fresh from the laundry.

The handkerchiefs were exactly alike so far as make and marking were concerned.

Hodge acknowledged that the handkerchief from the laundry belonged to him, and he did not deny that the other might be his.

Then he was given the opportunity to prove an alibi.

Hodge was cool and calm, as he arose, saying:

"In order for me to establish my innocence clearly, gentlemen, I will have to ask Mr. Merriwell a few questions. Have I permission to do so?"

Frank nodded and Professor Gunn gave permission.

"At what time did you leave the academy grounds on Saturday evening, Mr. Merriwell?"

"I do not know exactly---some time between six and seven o'clock, I suppose," was the reply.

"You walked to Fardale Village?"

"I did."

"Alone?"

"No," said Frank, blushing a bit, yet speaking distinctly and steadily; "I accompanied a young lady."

"I presume you walked slowly?"

"We did."

"It is a full mile to Fardale, is it not?"

"Just about, I believe."

"And you may have taken thirty minutes to walk it?"

"Yes, possibly more."

"Did you return immediately?"

"No; I stopped to chat a few minutes at the young lady's door."

"In this way you consumed considerable time--- possibly an hour? I mean in walking over and in chatting with her at the door."

"Yes, possibly an hour."

"Had the sun set before you reached her home?"

"Yes."

"Was it dark when you started to return to camp?"

"Quite dark."

"And it was very dark when you were attacked?"

"Yes; the sky was overcast, and that made it

very dark early in the evening."

At this point Bart produced an almanac from his pocket, turning to the attentive professors, as he said:

"You will please note, sirs, that on last Saturday the sun set at seven-forty-three. Mr. Merriwell has stated that the sun had set before he reached the home of the young lady. It surely could not have been very dark before eight o'clock, or even later."

"Very clear---very," nodded High Jinks, gravely, speaking in a thin, high-pitched voice---a voice that sometimes suddenly shot off into a squeak that was liable to astonish and startle a stranger.

"Very," agreed little Hot Scotch, in a deep, rumbling voice that seemed suitable for a giant.

"Saturday evening, from eight until nine, the band gave a concert," said Hodge. "What time was it when you reached the camp, Mr. Merriwell?"

"Just after the concert was finished," replied Frank.

"Or a few minutes after nine?"

"Yes, sir."

"How long before that did the assault and robbery occur?"

"Possibly thirty minutes."

"Very good," smiled Bart, thoroughly satisfied. "I am now going to prove that I was in camp, listening to the concert from eight until nine o'clock. Having taken part in the sports during the afternoon, I was tired, and I did not move about any during that time. There were others who felt the same as myself. One was Mr. Davis, here, who sat at my side and chatted with me throughout the entire concert. Is that statement true, Mr. Davis?"

Davis said it was.

"Another," continued Bart, "is Lieutenant Swift,

who sat directly behind me, and must have noticed me. Did you observe me, Mr. Swift?''

''I did,'' replied the young cadet officer promptly, for, although he did not like Bart, he was more than ready to aid in clearing the fellow of such a serious charge, in case he was not guilty. ''I noticed you several times during the concert.''

''You did not see me leave the locality, sir?''

''I am sure you did not.''

''That should be enough,'' smiled Hodge triumphantly; ''but Corporal Burrage was talking with Mr. Swift. It is possible he observed me?''

''I did,'' said Walter Burrage, who was the brother of Inza Burrage and the friend of Merriwell so far as a yearling may be friendly with a plebe.

''And you did not see me leave the locality?''

''No, sir.''

Hodge was now very dignified. His manner plainly said that he had been falsely suspected, and somebody owed him an apology.

''To clinch the matter,'' he went on, ''I will call on Mr. Gray, who is a particular friend of Mr. Merriwell. Mr. Gray sat on the opposite side of me from Mr. Davis, and, although we did not exchange any words, I am quite sure he noticed me. Did you not, Mr. Gray?''

''I did, sir,'' nodded Ned Gray.

''And, once more, did you see me leave the locality during the time the concert lasted?''

''No, sir.''

''That is all,'' said Hodge, loftily. ''I have clearly proved an alibi. It will be seen that I have been very unfairly and unjustly suspected. I have not the least idea in the world how my handkerchief---came in the possession of the person or persons who robbed Mr. Merriwell. I have nothing

more to say about the matter." And he sat down with
great dignity.

CHAPTER XXXIII

FRANK CREATES A COMMOTION

Of those assembled, Lieutenant Gordan was the
only one who did not look satisfied.

The officer's face wore a strange expression,
but he said nothing.

Strange to say, Frank Merriwell seemed the most
relieved of anyone present.

In fact, Merriwell's generous heart had not felt
at all elated at discovering that Hodge was the owner
of the telltale handkerchief. Hodge was an enemy, it
is true, but of late he had been very much scorned
among the cadets, and it was not Frank's desire
to "kick a fellow when he is down."

Still he would not have felt any qualms had it been
proved that Hodge was guilty, even though expulsion
for the dark-haired lad must have followed such
proof.

If Hodge were innocent, Frank desired all along
that he should prove it, and, now that Bart had established an alibi, he felt like rushing over and shaking
his hand.

This impulse he restrained; but he decided that he
must relieve his feelings some way.

Being a very good mimic and amateur ventriloquist, he decided to have some sport at the expense
of the two under-professors.

High Jinks and Hot Scotch were both bachelors,
but both had been smitten by the charms of a rather
frisky widow who lived in Fardale village.

The widow's name was Nancy Cobb, and she had encouraged both Scotch and Jenks, plainly hoping to capture one of them.

The boys of the academy were well-posted in regard to the situation, and they had been able to secure a little sport from it.

Now Frank "threw" his voice in such a manner that High Jenks seemed to suddenly squeak:

"Perhaps Professor Scotch may have observed Mr. Merriwell in the village Saturday night, as he was there looking after his girl."

"Eh?" roared the little redheaded professor, bristling up and turning fiercely on his tall, lank companion. "What did you say, sir?"

Jenks looked astounded.

"I didn't say a word," he piped, instantly.

"Yes, you did!" bellowed the little man. "You said---"

"Gentlemen!" cried Professor Gunn; "be silent! I am astonished that you should make such a display before those present. Discipline is the first law of this academy, and I mean to enforce it or see that it is enforced on any and all occasions. If you have any private bickerings, settle them in private."

"Oh, go bag your head!" said a voice that was a strange combination of Jenk's squeak and Scotch's roar.

"What's that?" shouted the head professor, jumping into the air and glaring at his assistants, who trembled and cowered before him. "Which of you said that?"

"It wasn't I, sir," quavered Jenks.

"Nor I," rumbled Scotch.

"But it was one or both of you," persisted Professor Gunn.

"I didn't open my mouth," asserted Jenks.

"I did not speak, sir," assured Scotch.

166

Professor Gunn looked puzzled and angry.

"I scarcely think my hearing is so much at fault as all that," he said, with great dignity. "I heard one or both of you retort to me in a very disrespectful and slangy manner."

"Rats!"

The word began in a deep rumble, and ended in a squeak.

Professor Gunn nearly fell over backward. Never before in his experience had anything of the kind happened. On all occasions his two assistants had seemed exceedingly polite and respectful in their demeanor toward him.

"This is disgraceful!" he cried---"disgraceful----infamous!"

"Oh, come off your perch!"

The head professor sprang forward and pointed straight at Scotch.

"You said that!" he cried. "You can't deny it!"

"But I do deny it, sir--I did not say a word."

The man's teeth were chattering, and he was the perfect picture of terror.

"He's crazy," Jenks seemed to declare---"he's stuck on old Aunt Cobb, and that's made him crazy."

That was altogether too much for the red-haired professor. Up he shot, like a rocket, beating the air with his clenched fists, as he bellowed:

" 'Old Aunt Cobb!' The lady is twenty years his junior! Everybody heard him then! Dignity or no dignity, I will defend a lady! I'll challenge Mr. Jenks to a death duel! This matter shall be settled on the field of honor!"

"Silence! silence! silence!" shouted Professor Gunn, growing purple. "If this does not cease immediately, I will have you both removed from your positions by the board of directors. I believe you are crazy, both of you!"

The threat was enough to make both Scotch

and Jenks collapse into their seats, where they sat glaring at each other and trembling with mingled apprehension and anger.

To those who were witnessing this scene it seemed comical in the extreme, and it was with great difficulty that the boys kept from shouting with laughter. Looking at each other out of the corners of their eyes, the two enraged professors held their hands low down by their sides, so Professor Gunn could not see them, and shook them menacingly at each other.

Probably the most disgusted person present was Lieutenant Gordan, whose appreciation of humor was small, and whose ideas of discipline and respectful display were rigid.

"This is what comes of such unofficial investigations," he muttered, angrily. "They do more injury to the academy than anything else possibly could. And still it is Professor Gunn's boast that the school is modeled accurately after West Point!"

He arose and left the room, his manner expressing his feelings fully as well as if he had spoken out plainly.

Professor Gunn stood glaring at his two assistants and breathing heavily. Plainly, his feelings were too outraged for words. A deep silence fell on the room.

It was broken by the squeaking of a rat.

Now, if there was anything in the wide world that could make the hair that surrounded the bald spot on Zenas Gunn's head stand erect, it was a rat.

He hated and feared rats with all the intensity of his nature, and he showed symptoms of alarm at the first squeak.

Squeak! squeak! squeak!

Professor Gunn grasped a pointer, and, beginning to quiver from head to feet, sprang up on a chair, after the style of a woman who has been frightened by a mouse.

"Hear that!" he cried. "It's a rat! Hear it! He's close around here somewhere. Kill him--- kill the beast! Don't let him touch me!"

Scotch and Jenks jumped up and looked about for the rat, both eager to kill the creature, and thus restore themselves in favor with Professor Gunn.

"Young gentlemen," said the professor, appealingly, "Will you be good enough to assist in the destruction of this rat?"

"Order out a battalion!" Hot Scotch seemed to roar.

"Arm them with squirt - guns!" High Jinks seemed to squeal.

"This is no time for levity!" snarled Professor Gunn. "Can't you hear that rat squeaking for me? There---there! Hear him! He must be right under this chair!"

Then the alarmed professor made frantic efforts to crawl up on the back of the chair, so he might be still higher from the floor. In doing this he lost his balance, pitched heavily upon High Jinks, whom he clutched frantically about the slender neck.

The head professor was somewhat corpulent, and Jenks was not muscular.

Down they went, and it happened that little Hot Scotch was underneath.

They flattened him out on the floor in a most alarming manner, bringing a roar from his lips such as might have escaped a giant.

The boys rushed forward and dragged them apart, but the little professor was completely done up.

In the meantime it seemed that the rat had escaped, for he was not heard again, and the excitement gradually subsided.

CHAPTER XXXIV

HODGE GROWS DESPERATE

"Look here, Merriwell," said Ned Gray, draw-ing him aside as they were returning to camp, "I am dead onto you."

"What do you mean?" asked Frank.

"You made the squeaking that Old Gunn thought was a rat. Now, you can't deny it."

"All right, if you say so," smiled Frank. "I don't like to contradict a friend."

"Well, wasn't it you? Now, be honest?"

"Possibly."

"I knew it!" cried Ned, slapping his thigh. "You are a funny guy, Merriwell! Now I tumble to something else."

"Is that so?"

"Sure. Twice when High Jinks and Hot Scotch seemed to say something I did not see their lips move."

"Well?"

"I don't believe they made half the talk Old Gunn thought they did. You were at the bottom of it, Frank Merrewell! You are a ventriloquist!"

Frank said nothing, but he was not pleased to have Gray discover the truth, for he knew it might get out and so cause him serious trouble.

Ned was studying Frank's face closely, and he was swift to detect the cloud upon it. Being a bright lad, he immediately divined the cause of the shadow, and he said:

"Now, you needn't be afraid that I will squeal on you, Merriwell. I am not that kind of a fellow, and I like fun too well myself. By Jove! you are funny!"

Then Frank thought it best to make a "clean breast" and bind Ned to secrecy, which he did.

The two lads laughed heartily over the row Frank had brought about, and the situation seemed far more comical to Ned when he understood that Scotch and Jenks had not said half the offensive things to each other that they were supposed to say.

"You're a genius, Merriwell!" chuckled Ned. "You'll be the ruin of this school if you keep on. Why, such a thing as an open quarrel between the professors is unheard of! It will be nuts for the fellows!"

Then Ned spoke of Hodge, whom he cordially disliked.

"It is sure enough that fellow was not in the crowd that robbed you, Merriwell," he said. "He's none too good for a job like that; but he kept out this time."

"That being the case, I am glad he proved his innocence," said Frank, heartily. "I don't want to see any fellow punished for something he didn't do, even though he is an enemy to me."

"You are always generous, old man."

"I try to be just, at least."

That night, immediately after supper, as Hodge was standing in front of the tent, Leslie Gage came up.

"Mr. Hodge," he said, "my friend, Mr. Hawkins, demands an apology from you."

Hodge whistled.

"So you are Hawkins' second!" he sneered. "I did have an idea that I could count on you as a friend. You have been willing enough to share

171

what my money bought.''

Gage colored, and then hotly returned:

''Have a care, plebe, or you will find another fight on your hands when Hawkins is through with you! You are altogether too free with your tongue.''

''Oh, am I!'' retorted Hodge, with spirit. ''Well, I am not afraid of Hawkins, yourself, or your whole company. I will fight you both, one after the other, and I'll fight at any time and any place you may name!''

Frank Merriwell had come to the front of the tent, and he felt like applauding Hodge. For the first time since they had met, he felt a touch of admiration for the proud-spirited, dark-haired lad.

Barney Mulloy gasped with astonishment:

''That do beat the Dutch!''

''Vell, I dunno about dat,'' said Hans. ''Maybe I do better as dat if I vas in his place?''

''Oh, all right, my hearty!'' returned Gage, angrily. ''I rather think Hawkins will give you all you need, and you will be only too glad to apologize to me then.''

At this moment, seeing something was up, Hugh Bascomb came toward the spot.

''What's the row here, Mr. Hodge?'' he asked, gruffly, glaring at Gage. ''Who is looking for a fight? Can I serve you, Mr. Hodge?''

Bart hesitated, colored, glanced swiftly at his tent-mates, and then said:

''Yes, you can act as my second, Mr. Bascomb. I have to meet Mr. Hawkins. I will leave you to make arrangements with Mr. Gage.''

Then he walked away, and left the two together.

''By Jove!'' said Frank, in a low tone, to Barney, ''I am really ashamed! It is pretty hard when a fellow has to go outside his tent-mates for a second.''

"That's so," confessed the Irish boy; "but Hodge has never a soul but himself to blame at all, at all."

"That is true enough, perhaps. However, it was plain he did not accept Bascomb from choice. He appeared rather ashamed to be forced into taking him at all. Bascomb is a coarse, cheap fellow, and Hodge has good blood in his veins, for all of his record. He is no coward when it comes to a fight, and I do not believe he is unusually cowardly under any circumstances, though he is easily rattled, and loses his head."

"Ya're too easy wid him, Frankie, boy. Why, if he had done to some fellas what he has to ya, the'd never rest until they had squared wid him."

"Oh, what's the use to hold a grudge like that. I am going to see this fight, and I hope Hodge will lick Hawkins."

That evening a number of the cadets succeeded in leaving the grounds on various excuses, some dodged the sentries, and at least fifty fellows escaped in one way or another.

They were all headed for the old boathouse down the Cove.

Not many of the plebes knew of the impending fight, but Frank, Barney, and Hans found a way to be on hand.

It was an excited mob that gathered in the boathouse, at the windows of which three thicknesses of old sails had been hung, so the light might not be seen on the outside.

Again, through his second, Hawkins demanded an apology from Hodge, but the dark-haired boy simply laughed at him, and then they stripped.

Hawkins showed up splendidly. His flesh was hard and firm, and the muscles of his arms, back and chest stood out plainly in folds, telling that he had trained to a point that was little short of

173

perfection. He was confident of "doing" the plebe with very little trouble.

It seemed that Hawkins had a record as a fighter, and Hodge was told over and over that he had insulted the best man in the whole corps.

Bart's face was gray and hard, and his eyes blazing. He said very little, but he had a sort of do-or-die look that seemed to indicate that he meant to win the fight if it lay in him.

He did not show up so well when he had stripped to the waist, although he seemed supple and sinewy. Plainly he lacked the advantage Hawkins had received by long and steady training.

But the two lads were going into the fight in entirely different moods. Hawkins was confident, as he had never been whipped by anyone since entering the school, and he knew that, considering the training he had received, he should be scientifically, as well as physically, Hodge's superior.

On the other hand, Hodge was desperate, although wonderfully cool. In his heart he seemed to feel as it if were a matter of life or death with him. Of late he had been under a cloud; if he could whip Hawkins, he fancied the cloud would lift. And he felt that the cloud must be lifted if he remained in Fardale Academy, for his proud spirit could not endure the present condition of things.

He would fight like a wildcat, and his opponent was liable to meet with an unpleasant surprise.

Frank read all this in Bart's face.

"I am going to see that he has fair play," muttered Merriwell.

CHAPTER XXXV

FRANK SEES FAIR PLAY

There was a strained hush of expectation as the two lads came up to the scratch.

The referee gave the word, and the fight was on.

Hawkins was cool and deliberate, while it was plain to observing eyes that Hodge was holding himself in check.

Both boys put up a "guard" that was correct, and there was very little difference in the positions they assumed.

It was plain that Hawkins had determined to lead Hodge on at first, and so find out what he knew about "the art of self-defense." He feinted and rushed several times, but Bart remained cool, and was not deceived.

The spectators began to show impatience.

"Come, come, Hawkins!" somebody called; "are you going to fool with that plebe all night?"

"Sail in lively and finish the fight," adivsed another. "We can't stay here long, you know."

It seemed that Hawkins decided to take his advice, for he began to force the fighting.

As Hodge had shown no skill in getting after him when feinted, Hawkins decided that he could not be very dangerous, and so he was somewhat careless in looking after his own face and body. He crowded Bart back, and then, feinting with his right, struck a smashing blow with his left.

Hodge dodged a bit, but he received enough of the blow to send him staggering.

He came back at Hawkins like a leaping panther, his dark eyes flashing fire. Smack---crack--smack!

Three blows were struck so swiftly that the watching lads could scarcely tell who had delivered them.

Hawkins struck but one of them.

Hodge gave him the other two, one on the chest, and the other fairly between the eyes.

Both lads reeled backward, but Hawkins could not recover until he had fallen on one hand and one knee.

Hodge followed him up like an enraged panther, but the referee shouted time as Hawkins struggled to his feet, and the first round was finished.

Still the older cadet was the favorite, and one confident admirer offered odds of ten to one on him.

"I will take that bet," cried Frank Merriwell. "Put up your dough!"

That fellow was taken aback, but he quickly saw a way out of the trap, and so he returned:

"Up she goes---a whole dime. Produce your cent, plebe, or back down."

"Oh, come off the roof!" returned Frank, scornfully and slangily. "You give me that tired feeling! I thought you had blood, and really wanted to bet."

This might have produced more trouble, but, at this moment, the two fighters faced each other once more.

Hodge had not failed to note that Merriwell had offered to bet on him, and, for some reason, that made him more that ever determined to lick Hawkins.

But Hawkins had learned that his opponent was not to be trifled with. He resolved to go in and end the fight in short order.

The next round was a rattler from start to finish. Hawkins pressed Hodge, following him up doggedly, and Bart was hammered more or less, without getting in a single effective blow in return.

"One more round like that will finish him, old man," said Gage to Hawkins, as they were resting at the call of time. "Teach the fellow a lesson."

"Oh, I will K.O. him in short order now," was the confident assertion.

Bart was given no encouragement by his second.

"You're no match for that fellow," declared Bascomb. "He will hammer your head off."

Not a word did Hodge say in reply, but he set his teeth firmly, resolved in his heart never to be licked until he was completely knocked out.

Merriwell had heard Bascomb's words, and he said to Barney:

"It's a shame! I believe in giving any fellow a fair show, and I will bet every cent I can raise that Hodge's own second is against him! It is a conspiracy to get him licked."

"Well, Frankie, boy, ya can't blame them for not likin' the blagguard, can ya?"

"I believe in giving a fellow a fair show, whether I like him or not. But that is not it. Some of these fellows---Bascomb, for instance---have professed to be very friendly with Hodge, and now they are betraying him. It is nasty---that's what!"

Frank's face showed his disgust and indignation. He did not stop to consider the matter, or he might have known that Hodge had bought "friendship" with a free expenditure of money, and that kind of affection is never sincere.

Hawkins had decided to act on his second's advice, and he was doing his best to end the fight in the third round. For some seconds, he gave Hodge far the worst of it, but Bart was watching his chance, and, when crowded, he suddenly caught Hawkins round the waist with his right arm, passed his left leg behind the fellow, caught his right arm with a firm grip, and then--

Up went Hawkins' feet into the air, and down he dropped upon the back of his neck.

Hodge had given him the side-fall.

The shock dazed and benumbed the surprised cadet. The referee began counting slowly, while Hodge stood waiting for his antagonist to rise.

Was it possible Hawkins had been so stunned that he would be counted out?

No! He sat up, leaped backward, and was on his feet, ready to meet Bart again.

Thus ended the third round.

"For Heaven's sake, don't let him do that again!" gasped Leslie Gage, in Hawkins' ear. "You gave me an awful fright! I thought he had stunned you so you would not be able to get up before you were counted out!"

Hawkins grinned in a sickly way.

"I was trying to finish him then and there, and I thought I had him too rattled to clinch. He's got guts."

"I knew that to start with. I told you that you would have to go at him hot, and finish him in short order. He is not the kind of a fellow to lie down and be counted out after he has taken a little punishment."

Bart had been hammered rather severely, and his face was bruised and bleeding, but he did not seem to mind this in the least. He sat quietly with the blanket wrapped about his shoulders, allowing Bascomb to wipe the blood with a moist towel, and the gleam in his eyes told that he had not the least thought of giving in.

"It's no use, Hodge," said Bascomb; "you are getting much the worst of it. He will finish you next time."

178

Frank heard this, and it was more than he could stand. He had no love for Hodge, but he did have a love of fair play.

"You are a beautiful second, Mr. Bascomb!" he cut in. "You are trying to discourage Mr. Hodge. That is not right. He has held his own thus far, and you know it; Hawkins came near being counted out just now. One more fall like that will fix him."

"Bah!" retorted Bascomb. "You ought to feel proud of yourself! Not one of Mr. Hodge's tentmates would act as his second."

That cut Frank, whose face reddened.

Time was up, and the two lads stepped into the ring again.

Now came the hottest round yet seen. At the very start there was a whirl at "infighting," but, seeing Hawkins was getting the best of this, Hodge broke ground and retreated. Hawkins followed, making a rush, which the other barely succeeded in avoiding by a duck and dodge. On this Hodge came up under Hawkins' arm, and then he found his best opportunity. The blow he gave Hawkins in the neck would have knocked down an ordinary prize-fighter, and the older cadet measured his length on the floor.

"Vell, dat vas a corker!" observed Hans Dunnerwust, who had kept still until this moment. "I have never seen der beat of dat already yet."

Still Hawkins could not be counted out. He got upon his feet, but he was decidedly "groggy" to the end of the round.

Bascomb, for the first time, pretended to congratulate Hodge.

"By Jove! I believe you will do him yet, old man!" he said, as he wrapped the blanket about the shoulders of the heavily-breathing lad. "You are astonishing everybody. Here---have a drink of water. It will do you good."

He thrust a tin dipper into Bart's hand, and Bart

179

lifted it to his lips.

The dipper was suddenly dashed to the floor, and its contents spilled.

Frank Merriwell did it.

"Not on your life, Bascomb!" he said. "I don't know what you put in that water, but I saw you drop some kind of a powder into it, as did several others. I have proof on that point. I am here to see fair play, and I mean to see it."

Bascomb snarled out some fierce words, and would have made a rush at Merriwell, but he was held in check, while several said:

"Not here---now! Wait until after this first matter is settled."

"Oh, I'll hammer the face off that fellow!" grated Bascomb.

Hodge was a little dazed, but he realized that Merriwell had interfered in his behalf, and he declined to take a drink of water from anybody.

"I can go another round without it," he said.

When the two lads came again to the scratch, it was seen that Hawkins had lost much of his serene confidence, while Hodge was as determined as ever. And now Bart pressed the fighting, doing it in a way that gave the other lad all he could attend to--- and a little more.

The excitement among the spectators was at fever pitch. They watched every movement of the battling lads with breathless interest, for a better fight had not been witnessed in the old boathouse for many moons.

Hodge was like a raging panther. He darted at Hawkins from every side, and his blows began to tell, while he received none in return. The cadets rose up on their toes, for they saw the end approaching, and a most unexpected end, at that.

Bart smashed Hawkins on the nose, then he thumped him in the eye, gave him a terrible punch in the lungs, and ended with an uppercut that lifted the fellow off his feet and stretched him on his back.

And there Hawkins lay, while he was counted out amid the greatest excitement ever known in the old boathouse.

Hodge had won the fight.

CHAPTER XXXVI

THE MEDAL FOUND---ARRESTED

When it was all over, his blood leaping from the result of the affair, Frank Merriwell looked about for Bascomb.

The fellow had disappeared.

"He's gone, Frankie, boy," chuckled Barney. "It's me private opinion that he is a big shot. He didn't dare stop and meet ya."

"I didn't care to get into a fight with him," confessed Frank; "but I was determined to see fair play, and it looked suspicious when he dropped the powder into that water."

Now that the fight was over, there was hustling to get out of the boathouse and back to camp.

Having won, Hodge was surrounded by plenty of fellows who were eager to congratulate him, for all that they had expected and hoped that Hawkins would be the victor.

Frank would have remained and seen that Bart was properly rubbed down, but there were now enough to do that, and so, after a little hesitation, he departed, Barney and Hans accompanying him.

Hawkins was bitter when he recovered sufficiently to realize what had happened. He swore over and over that he would get square with Hodge.

Bart had little to say. For once in his life, he was not boastful, and he was rather cold toward those who had scorned him a short time before, but flocked around him now.

"A lot of sycophants," he thought, contemptuously. "I would give more for one fellow like Merriwell to stand by me than for this whole crowd that shifts every time the wind changes."

That night, a little while before taps, having got back safely to the tent, Hodge suddenly turned on Frank, saying:

"I want to thank you, Merriwell. One or two fellows have told me they saw Bascomb put the powder in that water. If I had taken it, I would have been knocked out."

"That's all right, Hodge," assured Frank, carelessly. "I simply did what I would want any fellow to do for me under the same circumstances. But I thought Bascomb was a particular friend of yours?"

"I thought so, too; but hereafter I don't take much stock in that kind of friend. I suppose he has turned against me since I refused to take a hand in---er---er---a certain piece of business."

Hodge's face flushed. It was well patched up with strips of court-plaster.

He did not say just what the piece of business referred to was, and he was not questioned.

For the first time since entering the school, there seemed something like a friendly feeling between Merriwell and Hodge; but neither offered the other a hand.

Hodge awoke the next day to find himself famous, for he had done something no fellow of the academy had ever accomplished before---he had licked Hawkins.

It would have been natural for Hodge to swell with pride and put on an air of great importance. In fact, it was difficult for him to suppress a desire to do so; but he thought:

"If Merriwell had knocked Hawkins out, he would have kept still and made no show over it. Merriwell is a pretty good fellow to model after, and I am going to try it."

So those who had formed the opinion that Hodge was a vain and conceited coxcomb were astonished to note that he neither boasted, strutted, nor acted as if he was proud of what he had done.

Perhaps Frank Merriwell was as surprised as anyone.

"Hodge must be ill," he said to Barney. "He isn't putting on any airs."

"Ill!" echoed the Irish lad. "Begorra! he must be sick enough to die!"

Of course both Hodge and Hawkins were obliged to "fake" some very pretty stories to explain the condition of their faces; and equally, of course, their stories were not believed, although they were not questioned too closely.

"Affairs of honor" could not be stopped at the academy, and it was thought best to be blind to them as far as possible.

Hawkins was sullen and bitter. A few times he repeated his threat to get square with Hodge, but, for the most part, he kept still.

Just before dinner, as Frank was washing, Lieutenant Gordan suddenly appeared at the tent opening, with an orderly sergeant and squad at his back.

"Mr. Hodge," said the lieutenant, in a tone that made Bart pale and shrink apprehensively, "I have been informed that you have in your possession an article belonging to Mr. Merriwell."

"What is that?" asked Hodge, huskily.

"It is the medal of honor granted him by the Congress of the United States."

Bart suddenly stiffened up.

"Then you have been misinformed, sir," he said, stoutly. "I have no such article in my possession."

"In that case, you must have disposed of it in

184

a very brief space of time, for you were known to have it last night---if I have not been deceived."

"You have been deceived, sir," asserted Bart, holding himself in check with the greatest difficulty. "Someone has been lying to you."

"It is possible; but I presume you will not object to being searched in the presence of Mr. Merriwell?"

Bart's teeth clicked, and there was a choking sound in his throat. To be searched! That was more than he expected under any circumstances. He was tempted to refuse, and then, unable to repress his feelings, he burst out:

"You may search me, but somebody shall pay dearly for this!"

Lieutenant Gordan stepped forward without another word, and began the search.

In a very few moments he produced something which he held up for all to see.

It was the missing medal!

Hodge gave a cry of astonishment and horror, his face growing deathly pale. If his surprise was not genuine, then he was in truth a very good actor.

"There is some mistake!" he cried. "I---I--"

"Silence, sir," came coldly and sternly from the lieutenant's lips. "You will be given a chance to explain before the court-martial."

Pale, trembling, crushed, Bart relapsed into silence, a light of despair in his dark eyes.

"Mr. Merriwell," said Lieutenant Gordan, "take your medal, sir, and guard it well."

Frank stepped forward and accepted the precious token; but his hand shook, and his face was fully as pale as Bart's. Not a word could he say, although he tried to speak.

Hodge looked at Merriwell appealingly, but Frank did not meet the look. He turned away, and something like a smothered groan came from Bart's blue lips.

"Mr. Hodge, you are hereby placed under close arrest and you will be conveyed at once to the guard-tent. March!"

Out of the tent Bart mechanically stepped, the orderly and the members of the squad closed around him, and away he was marched to the guard-tent, where he was to be held a prisoner in disgrace.

In less than fifteen minutes the entire encampment knew Merriwell's medal had been restored to him, while Bart Hodge had been arrested, and was in the guard-tent, awaiting court-martial and dismissal---or, in other words, expulsion from Fardale Academy.

CHAPTER XXXVII

CRY OF FIRE

"Fire! fire! fire!"

That cry ran throughout the camp the night following the arrest of Bart Hodge.

"Where is the fire?"

"It's the academy! Fire! fire!"

"The academy is on fire!"

That was enough to send the cadets leaping into their clothes in short order, and away they raced across the parade ground.

There was a reddish glow in two of the upper windows of the academy.

"It's in Professor Gunn's laboratory!" shouted more than one.

The professor was found on the steps of the building, wringing his hands and groaning.

"The building is lost!" he sobbed. "It will burn to the ground!"

"Not if there is a possibility of saving it!" shouted Frank Merriwell, who was among the first to arrive. "Where are the fire grenades?"

"I know!" cried Cadet Hawkins. "This way! Follow me!"

The lads plunged into the building, leaving Professor Gunn moaning:

"It's no use! The smoke is so thick up there that they can't get near the fire."

"How did it start?" he was asked.

"I was experimenting with some chemicals, and there was an explosion."

In the bustle that followed, Professor Gunn was thrust aside and lost sight of completely. Once in a while, his voice was heard moaning or directing the boys to save something.

The water of the academy was supplied from a pond some distance away, and the pressure was enough to make a good head. There was plenty of hose, and places to attach them on every floor. More than this, the academy had a regularly organized fire brigade, and the work of fighting the flames was begun in earnest.

The boys had no idea of letting Fardale Academy burn if the fire could be checked and extinguished.

As has been said, Merriwell and Hawkins were among the first to go bounding up the stairs.

On the floor where the fire was the smoke was almost thick enough to be cut into squares with a knife!

Hawkins did not hesitate to rush into the heart of this smoke.

"This way!" he called to Frank. "This way for the grenades!"

Frank followed him.

They reached the rack where the grenades were kept, and , securing all they could carry, they ran down the corridor toward the room where the flames could be heard crackling in a manner that indicated the fire had obtained quite a start.

The door of Professor Gunn's laboratory was thrust open by Hawkins.

To Frank's horror, a sheet of flame burst forth and seemed to completely enwrap the lad, who reeled back without a cry, and dropped to the ground.

Frank ran forward and hurled his grenades into the room. Then he caught up those Hawkins had dropped, and threw them also.

By this time he was nearly overcome with smoke, but he could not retreat and leave Hawkins there.

"I must save him!" thought Frank.

Hawkins' clothes were on fire in one or two places, and these spots Frank beat out with his hands, while his own face was almost blistered by the heat that beat upon him from the door of the burning room.

With a last fierce effort, he lifted Hawkins and staggered along the corridor, reached the stairs, and plunged downward, passing some of the fire brigade, who were coming up with hose.

Frank did not stop nor put Hawkins down until the open air was reached, and here he dropped in a heap, with the unconscious lad across his body.

* * * * * * * * * ** * * * * * * * * * * * * * * * * *

The academy did not burn. The grenades thrown by Frank Merriwell had checked the flames until several streams of water were turned into the room, and, for all of the smoke, the fire-fighters took turns at the hose until the last spark of fire was out.

But Hawkins had been seriously burned, and Dr. Brown looked grave, as the boy lay moaning with pain on a bed, his face and hands covered with bandages.

"It is my punishment!" sobbed Hawkins. "I am sure of it! I think I am going to die! I must see Bart Hodge. Bring him here."

So Hodge was brought under guard, still a prisoner who had been arrested for a most reprehensible offense.

"I am going to die, Hodge," said the boy on the bed, "and I want to make a confession before I go. I want Lieutenant Gordan and Professor Gunn to hear me."

The lieutenant and the professor were present, as was also Frank Merriwell, whose face had been scorched, and who needed Dr. Brown's attention.

"Hodge did not steal Merriwell's medal," declared Hawkins. "I stole it myself!"

"You?" cried Lieutenant Gordan. "What made you do such a thing?"

"Because I took a dislike to Merriwell. I tried to get Hodge to go into the scheme, but he said he had used Merriwell mean enough, and he refused to have anything to do with it. I hated him after that."

"But you were not alone? Who aided you?" questioned the lieutenant.

"I can't tell that. I don't want to injure anybody; but I want to do the square thing now. I was the one who took the medal from Merriwell's chest, and I had it placed on Hodge's person. There is no need to explain how this was done, for, as I just said, I do not wish to harm anyone else. I insulted Hodge, and he got the best of me in a fair fight. Then I swore to get even. So I had the medal worked onto him, and then I reported that I had seen it in his possession. Oh, it was a mean trick, but I am getting my pay for it now!"

"This is most surprising!" exclaimed Professor Gunn. "Then Mr. Hodge must be entirely innocent?"

"He is."

"Well! well! well!" gasped the professor; and that was all he could say.

Perhaps Bart Hodge was as much relieved as anyone. He had been crushed and overwhelmed by his misfortune, but a new light came to his face, and he now met the eyes of those around him.

Frank Merriwell stepped forward, and his voice was not exactly steady, as he said:

"Mr. Hodge, I congratulate you. Mr. Hawkins has acted like a man, and you are out of a very bad scrape."

"I know I have not always treated you just right, Merriwell," confessed Hodge. "But I hope you heard him say that I refused to take any hand in the stealing of your medal?"

"I did."

"I can't help it if I am not perfect," said Hodge; "and I have resolved to do my best to overcome my faults. You have used me better than the fellows who pretended to be my friends, Merriwell, and now I want to ask if you will shake hands and call the past buried?"

"Of course I will!"

And they shook hands.

* * * * ** * * * ** * * * * ** * * * ** ** ** * * * *

Hawkins was not burned so seriously as was at first supposed, and he was soon out of danger.

But there could be nothing further for him at Fardale Academy, and so he was allowed to resign and go home.

Hodge and Merriwell were the only ones who accompanied him to the station and bade him good-bye. He shook hands with them, and his last words were:

"Stick by Merriwell, Hodge; he's all right. I'm going to try school somewhere else, if the governor will let me, and I mean to be clean from this time on."

191

CHAPTER XXXVIII

CHALLENGED

It was midsummer at Fardale Military Academy, and the "plebes" who had entered the school some weeks before were now so well broken in to the ordinary drillwork that they made a very commendable showing.

The yearlings had grown somewhat weary of hazing, although it had not ceased by any means, and each older cadet had his particular "slave" to attend to the "drudgery."

By this time life in camp had grown to be an old story, and the boys were casting about for something to vary the monotony.

A group of cadets who had gathered on one of the camp's streets were holding an earnest discussion about various sports.

"In two weeks comes the annual ball game with Eaton," said Walter Burrage. "I wonder how our team will be made up this year?"

"Gage will be captain, I think," said Cadet Lieutenant Swift. "You know we lost our old captain at last graduation. He was a good man, but the team was weak in the box last year, and Eaton beat us thirteen to nine."

"What makes you think Gage will be captain?" asked Harvey Dare.

"Because he is a brilliant player, and he was captain of one of the strongest amateur teams in the State before he came here to school."

"But he is not particularly popular."

"It is not popularity, but playing, that counts in a game of baseball."

"I say," cut in another cadet, "it doesn't seem to me that the boys are practicing as much as they ought to. Why, they should have had the team made up long ago. It is team work that counts in a game of ball."

"That's right," nodded Swift. "That matter should be settled at once."

"We should have several practice games with the plebes."

"Yes, for there may be some material among them that we can use."

"Have you noticed Hodge's playing?"

"Not particularly; but Merriwell acts like a ball player, and I believe there is good timber in him. He might show up well in another year."

"It is not another year we care for. What we are bothering about just at present is this year. We've got to have a good team to meet Eaton."

"What position does Gage play?"

"He pitches."

"Who's the catcher?"

"Hawkins."

"Why, Hawkins is gone, as you very well know. It strikes me that our team is badly crippled this year."

Lieutenant Swift looked rather annoyed. He had not thought up to this moment that when Phil Hawkins left the academy the ball team had lost its best catcher.

"Harris will have to go behind the plate," he said.

Burrage smiled.

"You know Harris is a bum thrower," he said. "He is all right as a back-stop, but any one can steal bases on him. Why, with Harris behind the plate, if those Eaton fellows ever got to first, they would not hesitate to go down to second on the first ball pitched. No, no, Swift, Harris will not do, if we have any ambition to win this year. The Eatons are good base-runners, and we must have a very good arm behind the plate.''

Swift knew this was true, and he bit his lips in perplexity.

''I do not know of a good man to fill his place,'' he finally admitted.

''What are we going to do about it?''

''Tomorrow is Saturday. We must have a game with the plebes. After that, we'll have to settle on a team.''

''That's right. Where is Gage? He must send a challenge.''

''Here comes Gage.''

The cadet who approached the group carried himself with a superior air, as if he were fully convinced of his own importance.

''What's up now, gentlemen?'' he asked, with dignity.

''We were discussing baseball and the prospect of holding the Eaton's good play this year,'' replied Burrage.

''Beat them!'' smiled Gage, scornfully. ''Why, if our team is made up right, we will kill them!''

''If our team is made up right,'' echoed Swift. ''But there's the rub. It is not made up at all, and the time for the game with Eaton is close at hand. What are we going to do?''

''Get a move on.''

''That's right. Most of the old team is back, but we need some new blood. There may be some good men among the plebes. For instance, Hodge is---''

''What?'' cried Gage, in amazement. ''You don't mean to say you would give that cad a show on the team?''

''It is playing that counts, as Dare just observed. We want to beat Eaton, and, in order to have any show, we will have to select our best players, whether they are cads or not. Another

man who shows up well among the plebes is Merriwell.''

"If those fellows go on the team, you may count
me out," said Gage loftily. "I do not run with that
kind of a crowd."

"Why, what is the matter with Merriwell? He
is pretty popular with the fellows, and---"

"He may be popular with some; but there is
a time coming when he will not be so popular.
Mark my words."

"Oh, you have taken a dislike to him. You will
get over that pretty soon, the same as Hodge
did. Remember how Hodge hated him? Now he
thinks there is not another fellow in the world
who is quite Merriwell's equal."

"Well, I am no sycophant, and I do not care
to be compared with Hodge. That fellow makes
me sick! I'd think a good deal more of Merriwell if he had run Hodge out of the school. I've
got no use for softies."

"If you run up against Merriwell, you are liable
to find he is no softie. He is a fighter, and he has
guts, else Congress never would have presented
him with a medal of honor for bravery in twice
saving Miss Burrage from death."

"Oh, that medal business gives me a pain! I
don't see that Merriwell did anything great. He
is stuck on Inza Burrage, and she is stuck on
him so---"

"So I advise you to be careful what you say
about either of them in any presence, sir," said
Walter Burrage, sharply. "You may have forgotten
that she is my sister. As far as Merriwell is
concerned, I am ready to stand up for him anywhere and anytime. He is fair and square, which
is more than can be said for some fellows in
this academy who stole his medal from him."

"I hope you don't mean anything," sneered Gage,

with a sidelong look at Burrage.

"I'm not calling any names, but anyone who finds the coat fits is welcome to wear it. Phil Hawkins was more of a man than some fellows who are still in the academy, for he came out and made a clean breast of it before he left."

"Oh, he was soft! Because he was burned a bit in the academy fire, he thought he was going to die, and so he confessed that he had taken a hand in swiping Merriwell's medal. It's a wonder he didn't squeal on the fellows who were in with him."

"Oh, well, drop this!" broke in Harvey Dare. "This is not settling the baseball problem. Are you a pitcher, Gage?"

"Well, I was one of the pitchers on my team before I came here to school. We whipped everything that called itself amateur, and we gave one or two professional teams a tight go. I rather think I am pitcher enough for any batters the Eatons may have."

"Well, you ought to have a good man to catch you, and Hodge is the best we know."

"I will not pitch to him."

"Then we will have to find somebody else. We must have a practice game with the plebes to-morrow."

"Sure."

"They should be challenged at once."

"Now is the time to do it," said Walter Burrage. "Here come Merriwell and Hodge."

"Hodge tags along about him like a puppy," sneered Gage. "I should think Merriwell would get sick of it."

Instantly the two lads found themselves surrounded, while the cadet lieutenant soberly said:

"We were waiting for you. You are both challenged to meet members of the advanced classes

on the field of honor. Do you accept the challenge? Or do you show the white feather?"

CHAPTER XXXIX

BEFORE THE GAME

Hodge looked serious, but Merriwell laughed.

"We are neither of us in the habit of showing
the white feather," he answered; "so I suppose
we'll have to accept the challenge."

"Remember, this is to be a battle to the bitter
end," warned Swift. "Don't be rash."

"To the bitter end let it be," smiled Frank.
"Whom are we to meet?"

"I am one of the principals, and Mr. Gage is
another."

"Really? You say Mr. Gage is 'another.' Are
there still others?"

"There are, sir."

"How many?"

"Seven."

"Seven and two are nine," said Frank, with
quick intuition. "I presume we will be permitted
to select seven friends?"

"Oh, I suppose we shall have to allow you that
privilege."

"And, being the challenged party, we will name
the weapons---bats and balls."

"It's not easy to get ahead of you, Merriwell;
you have tumbled to the game."

Bart looked relieved.

"I didn't know but we had another fight on
hand," he admitted.

"Oh, we are not anxious to fight with plebes
when we can avoid it," said Leslie Gage, in a

way that was distinctly offensive.

"I shouldn't think you would be since the last time one of you fellows went up against a plebe," said Frank, in a good-natured way.

He looked at Bart and smiled, but it was evident that Gage did not take kindly to this observation of Merriwell's.

"You fellows don't want to get swelled heads because Hodge went up against something easy and came out best by an accident," he snapped. "There are others."

"If I remember rightly, it was said at the time that Hawkins was a great fighter--that he had licked everybody he had tackled. But we are not speaking of fighting now, but of sport, so let's hold our tempers. When is this engagement to come off?"

"How will tomorrow afternoon do?" asked Swift.

"That suits me. I will get together some kind of a team, and try to make it interesting for you."

"Oh, we don't expect the game will amount to much," said Leslie Gage, loftily; "but we thought we might get some practice out of it. Of course, you plebes won't be in it with us."

"Oh, of course not," smiled Frank. "We don't expect to, but we will do our best, all the same."

"And we may give you something of a surprise party," put in Bart.

Leslie laughed scornfully, not deigning to say anything further. That laugh was enough to bring a hot flush to Bart's cheeks, and he glared at Gage as if longing to strike him then and there; but Frank Merriwell's hand dropped on his arm, and he quickly relapsed before the silent warning of his friend.

"Then it is settled, I presume?" said Swift.

"We will meet on the field of honor tomorrow afternoon at two o'clock."

"That is satisfactory," assured Frank. "You will find nine of us ready for you at that hour."

After a few words more, Merriwell and Hodge resumed their walk.

"Thank you for warning me against getting into a rage with Gage, old man," said Hodge, as soon as they were beyond earshot from the group. "I am altogether too quick, I know; and you are doing me a great favor when you hold me in check. I am trying to learn to govern my temper."

"That's all right, Bart," said Frank, in his friendly way---a way that unconsciously drew others to him. "There's no use in getting into a row needlessly. I believe in fighting when a fellow has to, but not in fighting every chance one can. Gage is aggravating, but it is his way."

From that time until noon the following day Frank was busy making up his ball team. Hodge was to catch, and Frank would pitch. Barney Mulloy, who was a slugger and sure catch of all manner of thrown balls, was selected to cover first base. Sam Winslow was placed on second, and the big, ham-fisted fellow called Hugh Bascomb was assigned to third base. A lively little fellow, Sammy Smiles, occupied the territory at short, and the outfield was made up of some fairly good men. Taken all together, Frank believed he had made up a fairly strong team, and, more than ever, was he confident of giving the regular nine a "sharp go."

One thing Frank regretted, and that was that he could not find an opening for Hans Dunnerwust. Hans protested that he could play baseball in a way to surprise those who knew him, and, although he was fat and rather clumsy, Frank would have given him a chance had it been possible.

Every Saturday afternoon crowds came from Fardale village and neighboring places to witness the cadets at their sports.

Somehow it became quite generally known that there was to be a ball game on this particular Saturday afternoon, and an unusually large number of spectators assembled.

The regular ball team had a handsome gray uniform, with "Fardale" lettered on the fronts of the shirts.

The plebes appeared in blue flannel shirts and uniform trousers, making a good appearance.

Merriwell was very popular with the visitors at the academy, and he was greeted by a round of applause when he appeared on the field at the head of his team.

It was this very popularity with the public that made many of the older cadets jealous of him, and thus gave him enemies in the school.

Hodge had been one of the jealous ones in former days, but, from being an enemy, he had turned completely around and was now Frank's admiring and unwavering friend.

"Hear them cheering that stiff!" sneered Leslie Gage. "Oh, it makes me very, very weary! I will take particular pains to show him up this day, see if I don't. He won't get a hit off me, and I mean to hammer him all over the field."

Gage was a good batter, and it was believed he would find Merriwell "a soft touch."

The regular team had been practicing some time when the plebes appeared, and so they gave up the field for the latter to have their turn.

Merriwell took the bat and batted around, while Hodge caught and did some throwing.

Merriwell gave the word for every move and every throw, and, to the surprise of the older cadets, he was obeyed with a promptness and precision that told how utterly his men relied on him and were confident that he was the proper captain.

Hodge's throwing was easy and precise. The way he tossed the ball down to second gave the regulars an idea that they might not find it easy to steal that day.

Gage grew uneasy as he watched.

"We're not going to have any picnic with these fellows," said Swift.

"Bah!" sneered Gage, scornfully. "What does this work amount to! We'll jump on Merriwell and pound him to death in short order. He won't last three innings."

"Vat vas dat?" inquired a voice, and Hans Dunnerwust came waddling up. "Vat vas dat you heard me say? Merrivell don't last five minutes, or something of dat sort? Vell, I bet me yor roll dat he stays in da box der game out. Dat vas der kind of a hairbrain I vas! Here vas my United States currency, and I vill put der whole shooting match on him. If you has some money and guts, put up and cover dat."

Hans actually produced a roll of greenbacks, which he flourished excitedly around his head.

"Go away, you chump!" said Gage. "Don't you know betting is not allowed? You will get yourself into trouble, if you don't shut up."

"I'd been more pleased if you would put up," said Hans.

The practice was soon over, and the plebes came in from the field.

Then Frank won the "toss," and sent his men first to bat.

The regular team took the field. Gage sauntered into the box, and the game was about to begin.

CHAPTER XL

THE GAME BEGINS

The regular team had decided on the umpire, without letting the plebes have anything to say in the matter.

In fact, Leslie Gage had selected the umpire, without giving his companions an opportunity to express their desires.

He had chosen Watson Snell, a particular friend of his.

As Gage sauntered into the box, Snell broke the wrapper on a new Spalding ball, removed the tinfoil around it, and tossed the snowy sphere to the pitcher.

Gage caught it with one hand, stooped and gathered up some moist dirt from the ground, and gave the ball a good rubbing with it, in this way quickly soiling its spotless cover.

"Batter up," called the umpire, sharply.

Barney Mulloy was swinging two heavy sticks around his head, so that one would seem light when its mate was dropped. He tossed one of them aside, and advanced to the plate.

"Don't try to kill the ball at the start," said Frank, softly, as the Irish lad passed on his way to the plate. "Do your best to get on base."

"All right, me boy," was the reply. "I'll do as ya say, though I'd like to break Gage's heart by putting the first one over the academy."

Leslie struck an attitude in the box, and then, like a flash, his hand cut several eccentric circles in the air, and the ball came whizzing toward the catcher.

Barney went after it, and he missed by at least six inches, for Gage had given the ball a big "twist."

"One strike," called the umpire.

Gage smiled in a patronizing and pitying way, and then looked around on the spectators for signs of approval.

Barney grinned, as he lifted his bat and looked at it, saying, loud enough to be distinctly heard in that vicinity:

"Begorra! I don't see never a hole in it."

The catcher returned the ball to Leslie, and Barney prepared for the next move.

As the first had been an outside curve, the Irish boy believed Gage would expect him to be looking for another of the same sort.

"Just let him give me an inside curve, an' I'll drop it over shortstop," thought Barney.

Once more Gage made those bewildering motions, and then delivered the ball.

It looked a trifle wild at the start, and it was speedy, so Barney was given little time for thought, but he knew it was just the kind of a ball the average pitcher would use if he wished to send an inside curve over the plate.

So Mulloy swung at it.

It was a lucky swing, for the curve was exactly what Barney had counted on, and he did lift the ball just over the head of the shortstop, making an easy single.

"Wow!" shouted Hans, unable to keep still. "If dat Irish boy don't been born Irish, he vas a Dutchman, ain't it?"

Leslie looked disgusted.

"That was a clean case of luck," he thought. "I ought not to have cut the plate with that ball. Hereafter I'll trim the corners, and we'll see what the rest of those chumps will do."

Bart Hodge was the next man up.

He selected his bat with care, weighing and balancing it in his hands. As he went to the plate, Frank had a word for him:

"Advance Mulloy on a sacrifice," he said, quietly.

For one instant Bart felt like rebelling, for he believed he could hit safely, and it was his ambition to show up well in the game, as he desired to get onto the regular team. It seemed that Merriwell was making a needless sacrifice of him, and it was not his nature to endure anything like that.

But Bart was doing his best to overcome his natural inclinations, and he quickly choked back the words which rose to his lips. When he entered the batter's box he had made up his mind to obey Merriwell to the best of his ability.

Sammy Smiles now "opened up" on the coaching line down near first, and the way he worked his chin quickly set the spectators laughing. Sammy was quick-witted and jolly, and in less than a minute he had demonstrated that he was one of the best coach-line chinners ever seen or heard at Fardale.

Frank had signaled Barney to get what lead he could and wait for a sacrifice.

Gage tried to hold the Irish lad close to first. He made three snap throws over to first, everyone of them done in a different way, and each one came near catching Barney. Still the Irish boy continued to lead off, knowing the necessity of having a good start on such a sacrifice, in order to prevent a double play.

A sacrifice under such conditions was something unusual, and, by many, would not be considered good baseball, but it was because such a move was unusual and would not be expected that Merriwell had decided on it. Besides that, he had found out Hodge was a great "bunter," and a bunt sometimes can accomplish the same results as a long ball.

Having failed to catch Barney, Gage faced the batter a moment, and then, with no preliminary movements, delivered the ball.

It was a curve, intended to shave the inside corner of the plate.

Bart did not wait for the second ball.

The bunt was neatly done, and Barney went racing down to second, while Hodge did his best to get to first, or to draw the throw.

The third baseman got in and picked up the ball in time to throw Bart out at first, but the bunt had been successful, and, with one man out, the plebes had another man on second.

Gage looked more disgusted than before.

What were these fellows trying to do? They did not seem at all inclined to play ball in an orthodox way, for they swung away or bunted at the first ball pitched, and advanced the first man up on a sacrifice.

"Guten Himmel!" gurgled Hans Dunnerwust. "Here comes dat bully boy mit a muscle as big as a house! Just you vatch Frankie knock der cover off dat ball pretty quick."

Merriwell had advanced to the plate, bat in hand.

"If he touches a ball, I'm a fool!" thought Gage, who was beginning to get angry in earnest.

"Whoop-ee!" squealed Sammy Smiles, as he stood on his head on the coach-line and cracked his heels together in the air. "We'll have those fellows playing ball this end up in a minute---in a minute!" he repeated, with emphasis. "Wait until Merriwell hammers the leather! When did we ever strike such a snap as this?"

"Oh, close your mouth!" muttered Gage, fierce-ly. "You give me a pain!"

Sammy heard the words, and he instantly retorted:

"If I give you a pain now, you are liable to be in great distress before long."

This kind of talk was not allowable on the coach-line, so Frank silenced Sammy with a warning gesture.

"Can't I warble?" asked the little fellow, dole-fully. "Am I a clam? Must I cease to chirp, and allow my vocal organs to become corroded?"

"You are not allowed to address the pitcher, or any of the opposite players, sir," said the umpire, severely. "If you do it again, I'll have to put you out of the game."

"What if the pitcher addresses me first? Can't I reply to a polite invitation to close my mouth?"

"I have warned you properly," said Wat Snell, ominously. "You better be careful."

"Somebody bring me a plaster!" chirped Sammy. "I want it to put over this hole in my face, for I'm bound to talk when a gentleman politely invites me to close the orifice."

Gage had learned that some of the opposite batters were dangerous, and so, after making another snap throw to hold Barney close to second, he gave Frank a change of pace. The ball passed at least four inches outside the plate, and so Frank did not swing at it.

"Strike one," called the umpire.

Frank made a protest, but he was cut short, which made him not a little angry, for he saw that it was a case of "playing ten men."

Gage took courage, for he saw that Snell was bound to show him every favor.

The next ball, however, was so far outside that Snell was forced to call it a ball. This was followed by one that made Frank leap out of the way, and two balls had been called.

George Harris was under the bat now, and as

Walter Burrage had said, he was all right as a backstop. Up to this point he had not been called on to do any throwing, and the plebes were not aware that he was not a good thrower, and so Barney was taking no desperate chances.

But Gage seemed somewhat "rattled," as he threw yet another wild ball, which struck the ground a foot in front of the base.

"Ball three," decided the umpire, but his tone betrayed that he did so with the utmost reluctance.

It was now three and one, and Frank resolved to "take" the next pitch. Gage must have suspected this, for he sent a swift, straight one fairly over the center of the plate.

"Strike two," promptly rang out the umpire's voice.

It was now an even thing---or would have been with a square umpire. Frank, however, knew Snell was bound to give Gage the best of it, and so he determined to strike at the next one, if it came anywhere near the plate.

It was an outside curve, and it passed eight inches beyond the plate.

Passed?

Not much!

Frank had a long bat, and he swung at the ball, making calculations for the curve by reaching as far as possible.

Crack! Away sailed the ball.

"What a hit!" shrieked Sammy Smiles. "Run, you snails---run!"

CHAPTER XLI

THE GAME WAXETH WARM

A wild howl from the spectators drowned Sammy's falsetto, but he continued to shriek and wave his short arms until he grew purple in the face.

Barney Mulloy was a good runner, and he tore down the line to third like a race horse.

Ned Gray was on the coach-line near third, and he wildly waved his arms for Barney to go home, so the Irish lad cut as short as he could, and hustled in for the first run, crossing the plate on the jump.

By this time, Merriwell was going down from first to second. He could not tell just what had become of the ball, which he had sent somewhere into the outfield, but, depending entirely on the coaches, he kept straight on over second and ran for third.

The expression on Gray's face, together with his gestures, told that it was going to be a close play, and Frank strained every muscle.

The ball had been recovered and sent in from the outfield to short, while short whirled and threw to third to cut down the runner.

It was a beautiful throw. The ball came on a dead line, and there was a sudden hush, for it seemed that the daring runner must die at third.

"Slide!" screamed Ned Gray---"slide! slide!"

So Frank threw himself forward and slid head-long, with his hand outstretched for the corner of the bag.

Thump! the ball struck in the third baseman's hands, and he reached to touch Merriwell.

Too late! Frank was lying there covered with dust, his hand on the bag.

"Safe at third," the umpire was forced to declare.

Then what a shout went up!

"Hurrah for Merriwell!" cried the spectators. "Hurrah! hurrah! hurrah!"

"Vat did I told you?" cried Hans, so delighted that he could not keep quiet. "You bet me my life dat boy vas a slugger! You don't seem to beat him already yet!"

Leslie Gage seemed dazed. The third baseman tossed the ball to him, and he caught it mechanically. Then, with a sudden burst of rage, he jumped into the air and hurled the ball madly on the ground at his feet.

"Vat vas der matter mit dat fella?" roared Hans. "He don't seem to feel so vell as he might. And he vas going to feel a great deal vorse before soon."

Leslie was furious. How Merriwell had obtained a three-bagger off him, he could not understand. For some seconds he acted like a maniac, and one or two of the other players were forced to run in to calm him down.

While all this excitement was going on, Frank got quietly upon his feet and walked down toward the homeplate. He was half way from third to home before he was noticed, and then it was too late to stop him. With a merry laugh, he darted in and scored.

Then how the spectators did shout! It had been a long day since they had seen anything that delighted them so much.

Once more they cheered for Merriwell, and the entire plebe team gathered to congratulate Frank.

Hans rushed up and gave Frank a slap on the back, as he cried:

"Guten Himmel! nothing could ever beat dat!"

This stealing home was too much for Gage. He went into such rage that it was some time before he could be calmed at all.

"What are we---a set of stiffs?" he cried, grinding his teeth and flinging off those who were trying to cool him down. "Are we going to let those plebes beat us easy?"

"What's the use to get so excited over it, old man! said Roy Swift. "Merriwell is a slugger, and you can't expect to fool him every time."

"Hell! He hit that by accident. He can't do it again in a thousand years!"

"Well, cool down, or you won't be able to pitch another ball today. You are too excited to go on now."

"Excited! Well, if that wasn't enough to make anyone excited! Why, that ball was a foot beyond the plate! I want his bat measured. It must be four inches longer than regulation length."

"It is not, for I took care to measure it. It just reached the limit, and is not a quarter of an inch longer, so it cannot be barred."

"Well, if it can't be barred, it can be broken, and I'll find a way to see that it is. No more such accidents will .happen this day, if I once get hold of that bat."

The umpire gave the regular team lots of time, and Gage gradually became calmer, for he realized that he must do so if he was going to stay on the mound.

Sam Winslow was the next batter on the list.

Gage set his teeth. He could feel his entire body quivering, and he took plenty of time, gathering up dirt, rubbing the ball, and finding his position. The first ball he threw showed him he had entirely lost control, but still he hoped to get back in form in a few minutes.

Two balls were called, and then Winslow struck at a fairly good one, popping up a fly foul, which Harris easily caught, and two of the plebes were out.

This gave Gage more heart, and he settled down to business. With two men out and no one on base, he succeeded in striking out Sammy Smiles, and the plebes were retired with two runs to their credit.

"Now we will get square with those fellows in great shape," said Leslie, as he came in from the mound. "We'll make Merriwell regret he is alive. Every one of us wants to pound him."

Frank threw a few to Barney at first to warm up, being twice reminded by the unpire that the batter was at the plate. Harvey Dare proved to be the first man on the batting roster of the regular team.

Frank made no preliminary flourishes, but sent the first ball straight and fair over the plate, making it very fast.

As Frank had expected, Dare passed the first one, and stood with his bat poised, allowing the umpire to call a strike.

Following this, Merriwell sent in a couple of wide ones, and two balls were called.

Then he tossed up a slow sinker, and Dare went after it with all his strength, striking over it at least a foot.

Hodge now came forward, adjusted the chest-protector and mask, and got back behind the batter.

Two and two had been called.

Hodge gave the signal for an inside curve, and Frank put on steam and cut the inside corner of the plate, but heard the umpire rob him of his due by calling a ball.

"I'll have to fool him on another sinker," thought Frank. "That is the only way to get him to swing at it, and Snell does not mean to call a strike unless he is forced to do so."

So he gave Dare a sinker, putting more speed into it than he had into the other ball. Bart had signaled for a fast ball, but Frank had signaled back that he was going to throw a sinker, so the catcher was ready for it when it suddenly seemed to shoot toward the ground just as Harvey Dare swung.

Whiz! the bat encountered nothing but empty air.

Plunk! the ball was held in Hodge's big mit.

"Strike three; batter out," decided the umpire.

Then there was a great clapping of hands, and, among those applauding, Frank saw Inza, Walter Burrage's pretty sister, the girl Merriwell had twice saved from death. His heart gave a leap, and the hot color came to his cheeks, while he mentally resolved to do his best, knowing how her admiring eyes were watching every move he made.

Dare walked away from the plate, his face and manner showing his deep disgust.

"What made you let him fool you on that simple sinker?" demanded Gage, sharply. "You ought to have knocked the cover off the ball."

"Perhaps I ought," said Harvey, a bit sullenly; "but you know sinkers are my special weakness. I wonder how Merriwell found it out."

Swift was the second man up, and Gage urged him to do something. He said he would do his best; and that proved of no consequence, for Merriwell struck him out also.

"You fellows make me sick!" said Gage, as he picked up a bat and started for the plate. "It's my turn now, and I'll show you what easy stuff Merriwell is."

CHAPTER XLII

"BY FAIR MEANS OR FOUL"

Gage was confident and determined; he meant business.

Hans Dunnerwust had heard Gage's remark that he would show what easy "stuff" Merriwell was, and he cried:

"Don't you believe me! I have dat roll yet avile already, if you vant to talk business."

Leslie did not seem to hear this. He gripped the bat firmly, and fell into a correct batting position. He showed in his look and stance that he had no intention of striking out.

There was something about Gage's manner that seemed a challenge, and Frank was aroused to do his best. He resolved not to let the fellow have a safe hit, if he had skill enough to prevent it. He did not believe he could strike Gage out; that would be too much to expect; but he would keep him down as well as possible. At the same time, he knew he must make Leslie swing at the ball, for it was not likely Snell would call a strike on him unless he did.

"If I can get him mad, I'll have him," thought Merriwell. "He won't want to take his base on balls, and he will try for a long drive."

This made Frank believe Gage would strike at the first ball delivered, in case the ball appeared to be a good one.

Bart signaled for an inshoot, but Frank signaled back for an out-drop and Bart nodded that he understood. Merriwell's signals were so skillfully given that the opposite side was not likely to detect them. They consisted entirely in the positions he assumed when about to deliver a pitch.

Twining his long fingers around the ball, Frank suddenly delivered it, with a snapping motion of the wrist.

It started straight for Gage, but began a long sweep almost immediately after leaving the pitcher's hand.

Gage observed the sweep instantly, and he knew the ball must pass over the plate. He did not take into consideration the other movement imparted to it by the snap of the wrist.

With all his strength he swung at it, and the blow whirled him around and threw him off his feet, for his bat encountered no resistance beyond the empty air.

Bart Hodge seemed to dig the ball out of the dirt near one corner of the plate, for he was playing close under now, for all that there was not a runner on base.

"Strike one," came from the umpire.

"Guten Himmel!" gurgled Hans Dunnerwust. "Vat easy stuff dat Merrivell vas, huh? You vill see dat Leslie Gage knock der stuffin' out of dat ball I don't think!"

Gage picked himself up, looking mad enough to break something.

"I will hit it next time!" he grated, as he weighed the bat in his hands and looked it over, as if it had been responsible for his miss. "I was too eager to crack it then."

But, for all of his muttered words, his confidence was sorely shaken, for he had noted the wonderful manner in which the ball dropped.

Still he believed that Merriwell was nothing but a "sinker-ball pitcher," and one of the kind that could be hammered hard when the batters "got on" to his delivery.

There was just the faintest ghost of a smile around the corners of Frank's mouth, and that was more aggravating to Gage than a broad grin could have been.

"Oh, that plebe is a conceited hyena!" he thought.

He trembled once more with anger, and that made him far less likely to secure a safe hit.

Had he waited, it was probably that Snell would have found a way to call four balls, but he was so fierce to make a safe hit that he defeated himself.

Frank's next ball looked like a straight one.

Gage swung at it again.

Once more he fanned the air, for he had counted on a straight ball or a drop, and it had proved to be a riser.

"Strike two!"

The excitement was now at fever pitch.

Merriwell had struck out the first two men up, and it seemed that he might serve the third man and most dangerous batter on the team the same.

Sammy Smiles kept still with the greatest difficulty. The grin on his face was growing broader and broader until it seemed that he must explode in another moment.

Now Leslie Gage's face was ashen white, and there was a wild and desperate look in his eyes. He gathered himself once more, and stood up to the plate feeling like a person with one chance in a hundred for life---with ninety-nine chances for death against him.

"I must hit it! I must hit it!" he kept repeating beneath his breath; but he was no longer confident that he could accomplish so much.

It did not occur to him then to hold back and give Snell a chance to call balls.

Frank Merriwell seemed preparing for a special

effort.

Gage fully believed the plebe pitcher was about to try his most difficult combination of curves.

Whiz! the ball shot through the air.

Once more Gage struck, and, to his astonishment and disgust he realized when it was too late that Merriwell had finally thrown a straight fast ball right over the inner corner of the plate.

And he had missed it!

"Strike three--side out!" came from the umpire.

Merriwell had struck out three men in succession, and those three were the best batters of the regular team.

Gage turned away from the plate like one dazed. He did not rage and fume, for he was too stunned for that.

The crowd cheered, and Roy Swift was heard to say:

"That is the best exhibition of pitching ever seen on this ground---it was great head-work and wonderful control. If Merriwell can keep that up, he is a wonder, and he will become our star pitcher."

Gage heard it, and every word seemed to smite him on a raw and bleeding wound. His heart swelled to bursting, almost, and things reeled around him. He staggered a bit, recovering himself quickly, flinging off the attack.

"Become their star pitcher, will he?" was his thought, as he reeled beyond the crowd that was cheering and shouting around the diamond. "Not if I live! I hate him as I never hated a human being before, and I will prevent him from getting on the team---by fair means or foul!"

The look on his face was simply murderous. It must have betrayed his thoughts had anyone observed him then. All that was evil in the fellow's nature had been aroused, and he was ready for any black and treacherous deed.

CHAPTER XLIII

HODGE SHOWS HIS STUFF

"Whoopee!" squealed the delighted Sammy Smiles, turning a series of handsprings, as Merriwell struck Gage out. "All down! Set'em up on t'other alley! That beats!"

"I say, Merriwell," called Barney, "don't ya mean to give the rest of us a chance to do anything at all, at all?"

Hugh Bascomb was the only player who did not come in smiling. Bascomb looked disgusted, as he marched in from third.

"Oh, what are you making such a big deal about!" he muttered. "It was an accident. Merriwell will have a head bigger than a house if this keeps up."

He happened to approach Gage, and the eyes of the two lads met.

"What do you think of it?" said Bascomb. "Wasn't that great luck for the chump to have all in a streak?"

Gage knew that Bascomb disliked Merriwell heartily, and he also knew that the big third baseman for the plebes was not overburdened with scruples concerning the right and wrong of things.

"It's too much, Bascomb," he said, hoarsely. "Look here---a word with you."

He drew the big fellow aside, and they had their heads close together for a few moments. When this interview---which was very brief---ended, something. was seen to pass from hand to hand, and they separated quickly.

Frank came in from the pitcher's box, laughing quietly.

"It won't be likely to happen again," he said, as if making a promise. "We need some luck at the start. so we will have courage."

Inza Burrage was so excited that she longed to hug Frank right there before them all, but she held her exuberance in check as much as possible.

Hodge was not robbed of all the honors, for Frank complimented him on his efficient back-stopping.

It is true that Hodge felt more than one thrill of jealousy as he heard the crowd cheering for Merriwell, but he had resolved to overcome this inclination in himself, and he forced it down, trying to feel as elated as any one.

"My back-stopping may be all right," he said, "but you haven't given me a chance to do anything else, old man. I'd like to try a throw to second to see if I can cut a runner off."

"You will, probably, get chances enough before the game is over," assured Frank. "I am not going to strike out every man up, although I will confess I'd like to do so if I were able."

Gage took a drink of water, wet his temples and wrists, and then went down to the pitcher's box once more. The set of his jaw was like iron, and his face was pale as marble.

Was it possible that he, who had captained one of the leading amateur ball teams in the state, was going to be set aside for the plebe whom he hated?

Such humiliation would be too much to endure, and he had sworn to prevent it "by fair means or foul." Already he had taken steps. Would his ally be able to carry out the scheme successfully?

"If not, I will find some other way," he told himself. "That Merriwell shall not triumph over me!"

He was resolved to pitch for his life, and he

started in to do so, for he struck out the first plebe to come to bat, which gave him new confidence.

"I'll get it back--I'll be all right," he thought. "With Merriwell out of the way, I need fear no one else."

The second man hit a skipping grounder to short. It was an elusive ball to handle, and the shortstop fumbled it just long enough for the batter to reach first.

This error made Gage angry again, and he shot a hot remark at the fellow who made it.

Frank Merriwell was now on the coach-line near first, with Sammy Smiles over by third. Sammy opened up in his rattling way, while Frank talked directly to the runner, coaching the fellow to get a good lead. Gage threw over once, and then pitched the ball.

The next batter stood with his bat on his shoulder, as signaled to do by Frank, and took a called strike.

The runner had been instructed in advance, and he darted for second.

Then was shown the weak point on the regular team, for Harris made a bad throw, and the bag was stolen with ease.

This encouraged Frank to repeat the attempt, and he made two swift signals, one to the batter, and the other to the runner, both of which were observed and understood.

Gage, finding the base-runner was lively, made an attempt to keep him close to second, but all his tricks to catch the fellow failed, and still the runner played off daringly.

Once again the batter stood with his bat uplifted and allowed a ball to pass, while the runner scudded for third.

And once again Harris made a poor throw, so the base was stolen.

Frank had found out all he desired to know; bases

could be stolen at will on Harris. He made a signal for the batter to line out a hit. But it was much easier to make a signal than it was to make the hit, for Gage had no idea that the batter would let another good one pass without swinging, and so he began to send up "coaxers." Two of these the batter let pass, and then, growing too anxious, he struck at the third---missed it---was out.

Two men were out, and the plebes had a man on third. Gage resolved that the fellow on third should not score, and he did not, for the next man popped up a little fly to second base, and was out.

This was better, and Gage felt relieved as they walked in from the field.

"Now we must make some runs, boys," he said. "If we once fall on that fellow Merriwell, we'll hammer out a hundred without stopping. I believe he is cake, but we must find out how he crumbles."

The batter to follow Gage on the list was a good man, and the team depended on him for something.

Now it happened that Frank Merriwell, always generous, had resolved that Bart should have a play to show his arm and make known the fact that he was Harris' superior.

The first batter got a safe base hit, which did not worry Frank at all, as it was an exhibition game, and he did not wish to carry off all the honors.

His only fear was that the coach would not give the man the signal to steal second, and, to give both courage, he did not pay much attention to first, allowing the fellow to get a good lead.

Then he threw straight for the benefit of Hodge, making it too far away for the batter to get without stepping on foul ground.

The runner made for second, and it seemed that he would steal the bag with ease.

Then Hodge showed the kind of stuff there was in him, for he caught the ball as a hungry dog snaps

up a bone, and threw it with a short arm move-
ment`that did not seem to give him any effort at all.

Straight and sure as a bullet it flew to second,
going from Hodge's shoulder down to the baseman's
knees, which was the best place to catch a ball
and put it onto a sliding man.

The runner slid, but the baseman got the ball
and tagged the player at least four feet from the
base.

Then the spectators cheered for Bart.

CHAPTER XLIV

THE TIDE TURNS

"Hurrah!" cried a village boy. "You fellows with the uniforms better take 'em off and give 'em to the other crowd! They can beat you with seven men!"

"Vat's der matter mit you?" came from Hans. "You don' know vat you vas talking about, huh? Don't you know Leslie Gage was one of those fellas mit der uniforms on? He don't believe nobody can beat him around here."

"That was a beautiful throw, old man," said Frank, to Bart. "I don't believe they will steal more than a hundred bases on you today."

The next fellow lined out a long one, which was dropped by the left-fielder. But the runner did not try to steal second. He remained at first, and saw the next two men die without starting for a bag. The first popped a fly foul to Hodge, who made a nice catch near the screen, and the last one struck out.

At the end of the second inning the score stood two to nothing, in favor of the plebes.

The regular team was thoroughly angry, but they protested that they were "just fooling with the plebes," and would come off with flying colors at the end.

This talk, however, did not fool anybody who was familiar with the game of baseball, as it was apparent that, up to that point, the regulars had been more than matched by the plebes.

And now, to Gage's dismay, he saw that the strong

part of the line-up was coming up again, the plebes having hit around once in the two innings.

Mulloy was the first man to step up to the plate, and Mulloy was surely dangerous.

Gage resolved to be cool. He turned his back to the batter, and looked over the field, motioning quietly for two of the men to shift their positions somewhat.

Then he tossed his cap on the ground by his side, threw back his head, and turned about.

A second later, the first ball sped from his hand, gave a quick shoot in the air, and cut a corner of the plate.

"Strike one," decided the umpire.

The next two were so wide that the umpire was forced to call them balls. Then came one that was on a level with Barney's eyes, but it was called a strike.

The Irish lad smiled scornfully. It was apparent that he was to be given very little show, and so, deciding that Gage would be likely to follow the high ball with a very low one, he prepared to swing at the next, if it was within reach.

Harris came up, adjusted the mask, and got under the bat.

As Barney had anticipated, the next ball was a low one.

He nailed it.

Up, up into the air, and away flew the ball, while Barney struck out for first, the crowd shouting its encouragement and delight.

Gage's heart gave a great jump when Molloy struck the ball, and he turned to follow its flight with his eye. Then a feeling of intense satisfaction and relief came to him, for he saw he had moved one of the fielders to a position that was going to enable him to get under the fly. If he had not moved the man, the ball must have passed beyond his reach.

The man got under it...caught it...held it!

"Out!" clearly rang the voice of the umpire.

Barney was already running for second, but he heard the decision and stopped promptly.

"Oh, keep on running," sneered Gage. "You may as well run around."

"Begorra! it wasn't your fault that I didn't," quickly retorted Barney.

Bart was the next batter.

"Sock it," advised Frank. "You sacrificed before; swing this time."

Bart nodded. Then he came up and made an offer at the first ball pitched, as if he meant to bunt it to the ground just in front of the base, and try to beat it out to first, as the catcher was playing back.

Bart had bunted before, and this second attempt made it seem as if the bunt was his specialty.

Gage called in both outfielders and infielders.

Then he pitched a ball for Hodge to bunt, starting forward toward the third-base line the moment the ball left his hand.

But Hodge did not bunt this time. The first offer had been made with the intention of deceiving, and it succeeded admirably.

He struck the ball cleanly and, with a good display of strength, sent it into the air on a line that carried it directly over the head of the shortstop and into the "alley."

This time Gage looked in vain for somebody to catch the ball, and Hodge did not stop until he was safely on third.

He had duplicated Merriwell's trick, and done it with ease.

Now the spectators actually began to make sport of Gage and the regular team.

Before going to bat, Merriwell stepped toward the water pail to get a drink.

Bascomb was just taking a drink, and he dipped

up some water as Frank approached.

Gage's eyes glittered as he saw the big plebe pass the dipper to Merriwell.

"This game will soon turn the other way now," thought Leslie.

Frank drank, and then came to the plate.

Gage tried to dally with him by pitching him outside, but he lost control of one, and it happened to be near the corner of the plate.

Frank singled to center, and Hodge scored.

Then Merriwell stole second, and took third on a wild throw from Harris.

But he did not get home, for the next two men went out, one on strikes and the other on a fly to short.

The score was now three to nothing.

"Hold on, boys!" cried Hans. "Vat for you vant to beat those boys so bad for? If you don't let up already, dat ball club vill disband."

Frank felt strange as he entered the mound. His head was very light, and things around seemed a trifle blurred and hazy.

"I wonder what the matter can be?" he muttered, putting his hand to his head. "I never felt like this before."

Gage was watching his movements, and a smile of fierce satisfaction flitted across the face of the pitcher for the regular team.

"He will go to pieces this time, sure," he muttered. "I hope he will keep up long enough for us all to get a crack at him."

To the astonishment of almost everybody, Merriwell did seem to go to pieces, for the first man up hit safely, the next made a two-bagger, and the third sacrificed so that the first man, now on third, came home.

The regulars had made their first run.

"Now, you fellows who have been having so much

to say, just watch us pile up the runs," laughed Leslie Gage.

He advised everybody to hammer the leather hard, and all seemed to take his advice, for hits were made right and left, and two more runs came in, making the game a tie at that point.

And still but one of the regulars was out.

There was a look of wonderment on Bart's face, for he could not understand what it meant. He was signaling to Frank for certain balls, but Merriwell paid very little heed to the signals, "crossing signs" more than once, and sending in a straight, easy ball most of the time.

"What can be the matter with him?" thought Bart. "He seems to be out of it. I know something is wrong."

Then, with the ball in his hand, he walked down to speak to Frank.

"Ha! ha! ha!" laughed Leslie Gage, exultantly. "We've got 'em chewing gum now, boys! This will be a regular cinch from now on."

"What is the matter, Frank?" asked Bart, anxiously. "You are giving those fellows everything they want."

"I know it," was the husky reply, as Merriwell stared at Hodge with hazy eyes. "I thought I would come around in a few moments, and I did not want to leave the mound, for I know they would say I was batted out; but I guess you'll have to put some-body---else---in---my---"

He pitched forward, and was kept from falling by Bart's supporting arms.

CHAPTER XLV

HODGE EXPRESSES HIS MIND

"What's happened?"

"Merriwell's hurt!"

"He's fainted!"

"Bring some water---quick!"

Then the crowd surged onto the diamond and gathered about the two lads.

"Keep back, will you!" cried Bart, sharply, as he still supported Frank. "Don't crowd around us! Merriwell will be all right soon."

"But not soon enough to finish this game of ball," thought Leslie Gage, exultantly.

"What's the matter with him, anyway?" asked a voice.

"Oh, the hammering he was getting has made him ill," laughed Gage, sneeringly.

Hodge gave the fellow a dirty look.

"The hammering you are liable to get will make you sick," he flashed.

"What's that?"

Gage clenched his fists and started for Hodge, only to find his path blocked by Barney Mulloy, who said:

"I wouldn't bother the boy now, me hearty. If it's anything ya want of them, just look to me for it.

"I wouldn't disgrace myself by getting into trouble with you!" sneered Gage.

"It would be a disgrace to ya, for I'd beat the face off ya, me darlin'," chirped the Irish boy.

Leslie turned away, muttering fierce words.

Frank had not fainted, but his strength had left him, and things were going around and around.

"Help me off the ground," he whispered. "I think I must be ill. Perhaps I will come around all right later on."

Hodge's arm was about him, and Hodge's voice replied:

"There's something crooked about this, I'll bet my life! Come on, Frank."

The crowd parted for them to move along, and among those who watched them was a pretty girl with a pallid face, clasped hands, and wildly throbbing heart.

"Oh, it is so strange! What can it mean?" came from Inza's lips.

Leslie Gage had sauntered toward her, and was near enough to hear her words. He knew of her friendship for Merriwell, and he longed to supplant Frank in her favor.

"Excuse me, Miss Burrage," he said, lifting his cap politely, and stepping forward; "I think I can tell what it means."

"Oh, can you, Mr. Gage? I hope it is nothing serious?"

"Nothing very serious, you may be sure," smiled Leslie, insinuatingly. "It is simply a case of fake. Weak heart and weak knees. Merriwell was being batted too hard, and he lost his courage."

She gave him a look of surprise and indignation.

"It cannot be that you know Mr. Merriwell very well, sir," she said, severely. "He is the last person in the world to lose his courage. You should remember that he has twice saved me from death."

"I do remember that he has been thus far fortunate," said Gage, smoothly. "He is a very lucky dog for he has won your esteem and friendship. Now, if I could have had the same luck——if I had been

228

given the two opportunities to save you--"

"Could you have done so any better than Mr. Merriwell did?"

"Oh, I don't know as I could; but I should have been fortunate enough to win your regard, which I sincerely covet. But what has just happened must convince you that Merriwell is not what is known as a stayer, although he may do brave things by flashes. Look at the way I had to take it the first part of the game. I didn't give up, but I stuck to it. As soon as the tide turned and we fell on Merriwell, he weakened."

Inza was indignant.

"I refuse to believe that he weakened!" she cried, her eyes flashing. "He was taken ill---I am sure of it!"

Gage smiled indulgently.

"Merriwell is, indeed, fortunate in having such a friend as you," he said, "but I think you will find that most of the spectators will agree with me in thinking that he 'chickened out.' "

"I don't care a snap for that, and I think you ought to be ashamed to talk about him so! As a pitcher, he is your rival, and rivals should be generous. At least, they shouldn't say mean things behind each other's back."

"Excuse me, but I do not consider Merriwell my rival as a pitcher. I am the regular pitcher of the Fardale Academy team, and Merriwell is not in it at all. More than that, he has no chance of getting in. His pitiful exhibition of weakness today has spoiled his chance, if he ever had one. He is very fortunate to have such a warm friend in you, but that will not help his case with the boys who know him."

At this point the umpire called "play ball," and Gage excused himself, leaving Inza in an angry and doubtful mood. To save her life she could not help wondering if Frank had really been ill, or had fallen apart when he found himself batted hard, as Gage had claimed.

From the moment that Frank left the mound, the game had little interest for her. In fact, it had lost its interest for the spectators, as the lad who took Merriwell's place was "easy," and the regular team immediately obtained a lead, which they easily held throughout the game, finally defeating the plebes by a score of nineteen to seven.

Merriwell had been taken to the hospital, but the physician there could not find that anything in particular was the matter with him, although his pulse was somewhat above normal.

Hans, looking sad and disconsolate, hung about until it was reported that nothing serious was ailing Frank, and then he went back to see the remainder of the ball game. But he kept very still as he watched it out, and he took pains to get away before the last inning was finished.

"Dat Leslie Gage don't have a great deal of fun mit me, if I can keep out of his vay, you bet me my boots," he muttered.

Gage was smiling and triumphant at the close of the game.

"Of course we had to fool with those babies a little at the beginning of the game," he said, speaking loudly for Hodge to hear; "but we simply did so to give them courage. When we got ready, we sailed in and killed them."

"Which you never could have done had Merriwell been able to remain in the game," shot back Bart, who was boiling with suppressed anger.

"Ha! ha! ha!" laughed Leslie. "That must be intended for a joke! Why, we didn't do a thing but hammer Merriwell out of the box."

"You didn't hammer him out of the box, as you very well know. You did get a few hits off him; but he was so dizzy at the time that he could scarcely stand."

"Dizzy! Well, that is good! I don't wonder he was dizzy. The way we were pounding him was enough to make him dizzy. Why not own up that Merriwell found he was being batted, and flunked out?"

"Because it is not true. He is not the kind of a fellow to flunk, as you very well know."

"Well, he flunked today."

"You know better!"

"How do I know better?"

"Because I believe you know what really ailed him."

Hodge fastened his dark eyes accusingly on Gage, who showed some signs of nervousness.

"I don't understand what you mean," he said.

"Did you observe that the drinking dipper was missing immediately after Merriwell left the ground?" asked Bart.

"Why--ah---yes. I heard the fellows call for another dipper."

"Exactly. I took the other one, and I found something in it."

A bit of color left Leslie's face, while Bascomb, who had been listening, caught his breath and looked startled.

"Found something in it?" repeated Leslie Gage, questioningly. "What did you find?"

"I don't know yet what it is, but I mean to find out. It was some sort of a white powder which did not entirely dissolve in the water."

Not a few of the boys were listening, and Hodge's words produced an immediate stir of excitement.

"A white powder?" cried Walter Burrage, pushing his way to the center of the group. "Why, it can't be that you mean to hint---"

231

"Can't it!" exclaimed Bart. "Well, I am allowed to think, I presume?"

"Of course; and you think---just what?"

"I think Frank Merriwell was drugged during the third inning!" declared Bart, with his eyes fastened firmly on Leslie Gage.

CHAPTER XLVI

GONE!

"Drugged?"

"Impossible!"

The exclamations came from Burrage and Swift. Leslie Gage forced a laugh, and said:

"That's phony. We fell onto Merriwell's delivery, and hammered him unmercifully, which made him weaken. Merriwell has wiped his feet on Hodge in the past, and now Hodge is ready to crawl for the fellow."

"Frank Merriwell has used me far better than I deserved," declared Bart, manfully. "I know he has enemies who would not hesitate to drug him. There are those who were naturally much concerned when he began to show up brilliantly as a pitcher, and--"

"Now, I presume you are making a thrust at me, Mr. Hodge!" blazed Gage. "If that is so, you have missed the mark, for I saw at the outset that he was a very ordinary pitcher --- one who would go to pieces as soon as he was hit a little. He didn't worry me in the least. As soon as he saw we were onto him, he pretended he was ill, so that he might get out of the game. I'll bet he'll show up all right tonight."

"All the same, I propose to know what kind of stuff the white powder in the bottom of that dipper is," asserted Hodge.

"What do you suppose I care. I didn't have an opportunity to drug him, if I had been mean enough to do such a thing, so I am not worried about anything you found in the dipper.''

"You may not have had an opportunity, Mr. Gage, but I know there are others who dislike Merriwell quite as much as you do, and they would readily give you a helping hand.''

Gage could endure no more.

"You have made too much talk, Hodge!'' he flashed. "If you say I drugged him, or had anything to do with it, you are a liar! You are welcome to pick that up immediately.''

This was fighting talk, and Lieutenant Gordan was seen approaching the group.

Hodge started for Gage, his hands clenched, and an ugly look on his face; but the cadets quickly closed between them, and held them apart, while Barney said to Bart:

"Easy, me boy! Wait a bit, for the lieutenant is comin' this way. Ya'll have plenty of chances to cram the words down the throat of this louse. Besides that, ya had best prove that Merriwell was drugged before ya do anything more. That will make you solid popular, an' that's what ya want.''

Gage was easily pacified and drawn aside, so nothing further passed at that time between the two lads.

Bart immediately hurried to the hospital, where he found Frank on the point of leaving.

"Have you entirely recovered?'' asked Hodge, anxiously.

"Nearly so,'' replied Frank, "although my head aches somewhat. What do you suppose ailed me, Bart?''

"You took a drink while we were at bat just before the attack came on.''

"Yes, I believe I did.''

"Did you do it yourself?''

"Yes---no. Let me see. Seems to me somebody handed it to me, but I don't remember who it was.''

234

"I think I can tell you."

"Name him."

"Hugh Bascomb."

"Right; that was the fellow."

"I surmised as much, for Bascomb does not love you, and I have seen him talking with Gage several times lately."

"But, what if he did give me the water? You don't mean to say that you think---"

"You were drugged---yes."

A hard look came to Frank's usually pleasant face, and he said:

"I thought of that myself, I didn't remember that Bascomb gave me the dipper of water, and so I put it aside, and decided that I had no cause to suspect anything of the sort. It doesn't seem possible, but still---"

"I am going to find out, for I have the dipper that you took the drink from, and it seems to have the remains of a white powder in the bottom."

"You have the dipper---where?"

"In our tent. After I helped you off the diamond, you know I left you suddenly. I went and got the dipper then, and carried it to the tent, getting back to the ground before play was called."

"Good for you, Bart! If there is a remnant of powder in the bottom of that dipper, we will find out what kind of a powder it is. If it proves that I was drugged---"

"What then?"

"Somebody shall pay!"

"That's right, and you don't want to be too easy with the guilty ones, Merriwell. You are inclined to be altogether too easy. You could have kept me out of this academy if you had chosen, and it was no more than I deserved. The fellow who drugged you deserves expulsion, and he ought to receive it."

"He will receive something, don't worry," assured Frank. "Let's go to the tent, and have a look at that dipper and whatever is in the bottom of it."

Together they entered the confines of the camp, and proceeded directly to their tent.

Hans was there, and he welcomed Frank joyously.

"Vell, if you ain't a sight for sore eyes!" he cried , getting his meaning somewhat twisted. "I been worrying yourself sick since dat affair at der ball ground. Vat vas der matter mit you anyhow? Vas you caught mit a cramp in your head or something of der sort?"

"I was taken ill."

"So vas I ven I saw you go out of der box. Guten Himmel! dat vas too bad! I don't get over it in a veek. I bet me your life you vas done those fellas up if you had stayed in der box. They vas looking sicker as everything ven you vas taken off your base and began to put der ball over der plate right vere they vanted them. If you don't done dat, and you don't been sick, you beat those boys out of sight."

"How long have you been here?" asked Bart.

"I just come in."

"There was no one around the tent when you entered?"

"Nein."

"Nine what?"

"Nothing. Dat vas 'no' in German."

"I didn't know you could talk German," said Frank. "I thought you were a Dutchman."

"Vell, some things in German, and some things in Dutch are alike. Vat vas der matter mit you already? You don't been vell so quick as you believe you vas."

"There's no one around," said Bart. "We'll take a look at that dipper now."

"That's right," nodded Frank. "Bring it out. We'll make Hans promise to keep still about it."

Bart advanced to his bed and felt beneath the mattress, while Frank waited for him to bring the dipper out. A look of surprise came to Hodge's face, as he continued to feel around with his hand. Suddenly he jumped up and rolled the mattress back.

CHAPTER XLVII

BASCOMB ASSERTS HIMSELF

The game of ball between the regulars and the plebes created no little discussion.

Concerning Frank Merriwell, the boys seemed almost equally divided, some believing he had really been ill, and some believing he had faked illness as an excuse to get out of the box when he found he was being hit hard.

All who were not prejudiced admitted that he had seemed to start in to pitch a wonderful game.

There were a few who held that the regulars had been fooling with him all along, but they either knew little about baseball, or were down on Merriwell to such an extent that they eagerly grasped at anything to injure him.

Hugh Bascomb discreetly kept silent, after having once expressed an opinion that Merriwell had proved to be "cake" for the regulars, and found that his words were causing him to be regarded with keen attention and suspicion by some of Merriwell's friends.

Leslie Gage, however, was very free in expressing his utter contempt for Frank.

"Babies can bat him as soon as they catch on to his delivery," asserted Gage.

"What made you let him get a triple and a single off you in three innings?" asked one who overheard this remark. "If he can't pitch, you'll have to acknowledge he can do good stick-work."

"Oh, he got his triple at the start, and I hadn't

gotten warmed up; but both the three-bagger and the single were accidents.''

''It looked to me as if they were accidents you could not avert.''

''I don't care what you think; he couldn't do it again in a thousand years.''

''But Hodge kept up his stick-work all through the game. How about that?''

''Did you fancy I was fool enough to wear my arm out on such a game as that? After we had those fellows dead to rights, I let up.''

''That may be true, but there is one thing you cannot possibly deny. Hodge showed himself a first-class catcher.''

In his heart Gage knew this well, and had he not disliked Hodge so thoroughly, and had not Hodge and Merriwell been such close friends, he would have acknowledged it. To himself he had acknowledged Hodge was far superior to Harris. It would be to his advantage to pitch to the better catcher, and he knew it, but his hatred for Bart kept him from saying so.

''He did very well with the pitchers he had to hold,'' Gage said, loftily, ''but you must remember, my dear boy, that there is a great deal of difference in pitching. An ordinary pitcher sends in a 'soft' ball for the catcher---one with little 'stuff' on it; a good pitcher sends in a ball that is whirling with amazing speed---a ball that glances from a bat, making pop flies, fouls, and scratch hits. Such a ball is hard to hold, for it tries to twist out of the catcher's glove after he seems to have it fairly smothered. If Hodge had been back-stopping for some pitchers, he would not have shown up so well.''

''But his throwing---that is certainly great.''

''It is good,'' confessed Leslie, ''but he might not do as well another time. You cannot judge a man's throwing by a single game of ball.''

Sentiment, however, was strongly in favor of giving Hodge a trial on the regular team. If Bart had been at all popular, very few would have opposed him, but his quick temper and haughty ways had made him anything but a favorite among his cadet companions.

Although they endeavored not to betray the fact, both Bascomb and Gage were greatly worried. Hodge's declaration that he had taken a drink just before going into the box the last time, and that there appeared to be remnants of a white powder in the bottom of the dipper, was enough to put them on the anxious seat.

They knew nothing, as yet, of the disappearance of the dipper from the place where Hodge had concealed it.

Leslie tried to induce Bascomb to make a trade with Hodge for the dipper.

"You do the business," he said, "and I will furnish the money. Buy the thing at some price. Offer him fifty dollars for it."

"And I don't suppose you intend to show your hand in the matter at all?" questioned Bascomb.

"Why should I? You gave Merriwell the drug."

"And you gave it to me."

"Nobody knows that. Go ahead, Bascomb, and get that dipper someway. I'll make the governor cough up a hundred dollars, and you shall be well paid for getting the dipper and turning it over to me."

"You might pay me in money, and I might be expelled from Fardale. Oh, no, Gage; I am not going to play tool for you any more. I want to get hold of that dipper as much as you do, but I'll never say a word to Hodge, unless you tackle him with me. We are both in this, and you must face the music, as well as I."

Leslie restrained his rage with a great effort.

"You're a bull-headed fellow, Bascomb," he said.

"I didn't give Merriwell the drink, and everybody knows I had no opportunity to do so. I shall swear I had nothing whatever to do with it, in case I am rung into the affair, and you will have to run your own race."

"If I am exposed, I will own up to the whole truth, and you shall not escape."

Gage snapped his fingers.

"That for your threat!" he said. "Who stands the best in this school, you, who were known by several to be the leader in the affair for which Phil Hawkins would have been expelled if he had not taken himself out of the academy, or I, who have been here somewhat longer than you, and have obtained a grip. My dear boy, if you squeal on me, I will simply say that it is a case of spite---that, knowing Merriwell and I are not friends, you have tried to injure me. Nothing can be proved against me, and there you are. You will be expelled, and I'll stay."

As Bascomb listened to these cool words from his leader in wrong-doing, his face became drawn with rage, and a terrible look settled in his eyes. The cords on his thick neck stood out strongly, as if he were under a severe strain.

"So that's the way you'll work it, eh?" he said, hoarsely. "Well, let me tell you how I'll serve you. If I am expelled from this school, and you are not served the same, I'll lay for you until I catch you, and then I'll hammer you until you are so near dead that it will be hard to tell whether you have breath of life in your body or not. That's what I will do to you, my friend!"

Gage fell back, fear and rage showing on his face.

"Why, you big brute!" he cried. "You wouldn't dare do such a thing!"

"Wouldn't I! You may find out differently, if occasion arises. And now I want to say right here that I do not like being called a big brute. If you ever do so again, I will give you a good sock anyway."

It was plain that he meant it, and Leslie began to realize that he had formed an alliance with a fellow who might become exceedingly troublesome. He did not relish being talked to in such a manner, but he plainly saw it would not do to arouse Bascomb still more, and so he tried to soothe the fellow down.

"Come, come!" he said; "we are fools to quarrel. We can't afford to do so."

"That's right," nodded the big plebe, "and I am glad you realize it."

"I don't believe this business will be carried so far that either of us will be in danger of expulsion."

"I don't think it is best to have it carried that far."

"How can we prevent it?"

"By getting hold of that dipper, and making Hodge promise to keep still."

"Well, go ahead with the scheme."

"You must help me."

"How?"

"You proposed that the dipper be bought from Hodge, and that I do the buying. Now, I will tell you what we'll do. We will both go to Hodge, and try to get hold of the dipper some way."

"I won't do it."

"Yes, you will!" declared Bascomb, his manner growing dangerous and menacing. "If you refuse, I swear I will give you a beating now, and I'll tell why I was doing it, if you shout for help and call anyone up. That is business, and I mean it."

It was useless for Leslie to bluster or beg. Bascomb was inexorable. The sycophant was sycophant no longer; he was master of the situation.

CHAPTER XLVIII

THE SHADOW IN A HEART

And so it came about that Bascomb and Gage followed Hodge about that evening, and finally caught him beyond the limits of the camp.

Hodge faced them quickly, demanding to know what they wanted. He was suspicious, and he did not fancy being followed.

"We want to see you on important business," said Bascomb, hoarsely. "Is that right, Gage?"

"That's right," admitted Leslie, feebly.

"Name your business," directed Bart, still suspicious.

"It's about---er---that---er---dipper," said the big plebe, faltering. Isn't it, Gage?"

"Yes," confessed Gage, reluctantly.

Bart was interested immediately, but he held himself in check.

"What about it?" he asked, with apparent indifference.

"Well, we didn't know but we could make some kind of a trade with you," blurted Bascomb. "You and I have been friends in the past, you know, and we have done some things we would not brag about. Now, I don't believe you are the kind of a fellow to do an old friend dirty when he is in trouble. If we have harmed Merriwell, we are sorry for it. Eh, Gage?"

"That's right," said Gage, thickly.

"And we are willing to pay you well to give up that dipper just as you found it."

Hodge was not a little surprised, for he had supposed that, since the dipper's disappearance, it had fallen into the hands of Gage; but now it seemed that nothing of the kind had happened, and Bart wondered what could have become of the dipper.

"You are ready to buy it from me?" he asked.

"Yes."

"Then it is of value to you?"

"Possibly."

"It must be, and this is as good as a confession that Merriwell was actually drugged, and that you two fellows had a hand in drugging him."

"Never mind about that," put in Gage, with an attempt to appear superior. "All we want of you is the dipper."

"Well, you will not get it."

"We'll pay you for it," Gage hastened to say, growing humble instantly. "We'll pay you well."

"That doesn't make any difference."

"You won't give it up?"

"I can't."

"Can't? What do you mean by that?"

"It has already passed out of my hands."

"Who has it---Merriwell?"

"No."

"Then you have given it to Old Gunn!"

Hodge said nothing in reply to this. He was willing for them to think he had surrendered the dipper to the head professor.

Bascomb grew furious.

"That was a dirty trick to play on an old friend, Hodge!" he cried. "You have done things in the past worse than giving a little harmless powder to a fellow. I could have turned you in long ago, if I had been mean enough."

"How did I know you gave it to Merriwell?" asked Bart. "I fancied Gage was the one who---

"Gage produced the pow---"

244

"Stop!" gasped Leslie. "Be careful what you say!"

"Oh, what's the use! Hodge is the only one who can hear us, and we'll swear we never said a thing, if he reports it. He knows, and we can't fool him, but we can beat him up, and I propose to do it right now."

He took a step toward Bart, as if he would strike the dark-haired boy; but, at this moment, another figure advanced out of the darkness, and the cool voice of Frank Merriwell was heard to say:

"Don't do it! You may get hurt if you do. I happened to be near enough to hear all that passed between you three, and so I know now that I was drugged, as I suspected before. I also know that Mr. Leslie Gage was at the bottom of the dirty trick, and I will lick him at any time or place he sees fit to meet me."

"But---but, if I refuse---"

"You can't. If you do, I will slap your face in the presence of your friends, and brand you as a sneak and a coward."

Frank was terribly angry, as his voice betrayed. It was a singular thing for Frank Merriwell to betray such feelings, but the outrage he had endured had aroused him thoroughly.

"All right," said Gage, recovering; "I will fight you. But I must be given a little time. A friend of mine will see you later."

"Why not arrange it right here? I have a friend present, and so have you. It will take but a few seconds to settle it."

This, however, did not suit Leslie at all. He did not wish to be represented in a fight by such a fellow as Bascomb, and he did not want Bascomb to think that he objected to having him for a second, for the big plebe had an ugly temper, and he would be sure to lose it.

Gage was desperate, for he saw that he had fallen

into a bad trap. He had sworn to keep Merriwell off the ball team by fair means or foul, and the foul means he had resorted to had placed him in an ugly predicament.

Still Gage was not sorry. He hated Merriwell too much to regret anything. Now that he was being crowded to the wall, he felt that he could kill Merriwell without afterward feeling a pang of remorse.

He did not want to fight Frank with his fists, for he had seen Merriwell fight long before, and the plebe was a hard customer. Gage did not fancy being hammered.

But how could he escape? If he refused to fight, Merriwell would insult him publicly. There seemed no way out of the corner into which he had been forced.

"I'll have to meet him," thought Gage; "and I will do him up some way!"

So he got away as best as he could, promising to send a friend to meet Hodge and make arrangements for the fight.

CHAPTER XLIX

OVER BLACK BLUFF

Hugh Bascomb met Gage as the latter was coming from the gymnasium. Making sure that no one was within hearing, Bascomb said:

"I have the dipper."

Gage gave an exclamation of satisfaction.

"Where did you get hold of it?" he asked.

"Oh, Furbush, the drum-boy orderly, saw Hodge secure it, followed him to his tent, and saw him hide it under the mattress. When Hodge left, Furbush secured it."

"Where is it now?"

"Safe."

"I want it."

"Well, you may have it; but it will cost you something."

"I'll pay for it, as I said."

"But it'll cost you more than the sum you named. You've got to be more generous."

Instantly Gage fired up.

"So you mean to bleed me, do you? Well, I refuse to be bled. Now that you have tried the trick, I refuse to pay a cent for it. You are in the same boat with me, and if one gets into trouble, the other must. You may do what you like with the dipper."

"You can't mean that? What if Old Gunn or Lieutenant Gordan gets hold of that dipper?"

"We may both be expelled; but you'll have to go if I do. You have attempted to bully me lately, Bascomb, and I won't have it. You will find you have carried the matter altogether too far."

"Do you dare to cross me?"

"Yes."

"I'll make you sorry!"

"Go ahead. That's as much as I care for you!"
And Leslie snapped his fingers in the big plebe's
face.

Bascomb was furious, but he dared to do nothing
then and there, so he could only glare after Gage
and mutter, as Leslie walked haughtily away.

Merriwell did not know that Gage was watching
him constantly, as a cat watches a mouse it intends
to devour.

On the day following, Frank obtained permission to
leave camp. He proceeded to the old boathouse,
where so many fights had taken place and so many
plebes had been hazed, and there he secured a coil of
rope. With this he made his way down the shore
for a distance of more than a mile.

He finally came to wild and rugged spot, where
high cliffs rose directly from the water's edge at
the lowest tides.

Frank made his way to the highest cliff of all,
which was known as Black Bluff.

Halfway down the face of Black Bluff was a
rocky shelf, and on this shelf an eagle had made
her nest.

Frank had discovered the nest of young eagles, and
resolved to secure one of them to send to a friend
at home.

He made one end of the rope fast to a tree that
stood back a few yards from the edge of the bluff,
and let the other end fall over.

It uncoiled and reached the ledge.

Next, Frank removed his coat and placed it under
the rope at the edge of the cliff, so the rock would
not wear it off.

Having made these preparations, he swung over

the edge, and began the descent.

Far below the sea was rolling and roaring up against the base of the bluff, but he did not pause to look down there.

The eagle left her nest, and began to circle about, screaming her alarm.

Frank was about half way to the ledge, when he heard a shout from above. Looking upward, he was astonished to see the face of Leslie Gage, who was peering down at him.

There was a fierce look of triumph on that face--- a look that turned cold the blood of the boy who was dangling by that slender line against the face of Black Bluff.

"I have you now, Merriwell!" cried Gage, hoarse- ly and triumphantly. "You'll never bother me after today!"

Then he held out his hand, and Frank saw it con- tained an open knife.

At this moment Frank Merriwell was numb with horror, for he fully understood his enemy's murder- ous purpose.

Gage meant to cut the rope!

"It's quite a little drop down there," mocked the young man above, "and I think it will fix you all right. I swore to get you out of my way by fair means or foul, and I am going to keep my word now."

Then he started to cut the rope. To do so, he leaned a little farther over the edge, lost his bal- ance, uttered a shriek of horror, and fell.

Clinging to the rope, Frank saw the dark form of his enemy shoot past and go whirling downward.

It seemed that he had been saved by the hand of Providence.

Gage struck on the ledge, and lay there, motion- less, one leg hanging over the edge, his white face upturned to the sky.

"It is retribution!" thought Frank Merriwell.

For some moments he was too unnerved to do anything but cling to the rope. Finally, he recovered and continued the descent until the ledge was reached.

Gage lay there, white and ghastly, apparently dead.

Shuddering with horror, Frank drew his foe back from the brink, and then, unmindful of the screaming eagles and the young eaglets, proceeded to tie one end of the rope securely about Gage's waist.

When this was done, Frank summoned all his strength and determination, and climbed to the top of the bluff, where he rested a few minutes, and then drew Gage up.

From that spot he succeeded in carrying his unconscious foe back to the camp, although he was forced to rest many times in doing so.

Astonishing, and almost impossible though it seemed to Frank, Gage was not dead, although the doctor said he might be injured internally, so that he would not recover from the fall.

But the fellow was not even injured that much, although he was confined to the hospital for two weeks. It was one of those peculiar instances where a terrible fall is sustained without resulting fatally, or even breaking a bone.

But Leslie was in no condition to play ball when the day came for the game with Eaton.

Frank Merriwell filled Leslie's place, and Bartley Hodge supported him behind the bat.

The game resulted in a score of nine to three, in favor of Fardale, and when the game was finished, everyone but the ''sore-heads'' acknowledged that Fardale's battery was the best the academy had ever put into the field.

Burrage had captained the team through this game, but he immediately resigned in favor of Merriwell, who was accepted by acclamation.

"What are ya goin' to do with Gage when he's well, me boy?" asked Barney.

"Vat vas dat?" put in Hans. "Vy, he should make him one lovely fight before soon and break his face in."

"No, no," said Frank, laughingly. "Gage has been punished enough. The score is settled. We will forget the foul business and all the other rotten things, and let him try to regain his prestige."

"Vich same he never vill already," said Hans, excitedly.

"Not while I'm alive!" cried Barney, putting up a brawny fist.

"Come," said Frank, "not one of us would hit a man when he's down. Gage is down in more senses than one, and I guess, Hans, you're right when you say his prestige is forever lost. But let's agree to treat the fellow decently, and not harbor enmity against him."

Hans shrugged his shoulders.

"Vell," he said, only half satisfied, "vot you say, Frankie, it vas as good as done."

"And you, Barney?"

"Me boy, I am wid ya every time!"

"Good!" cried Frank, delightedly; "we're at peace with all the world."

The three boys turned their faces once more toward the cadet camp at Fardale. Many struggles, temptations, defeats, and triumphs were still in store for them, some of which will be related in the next volume of this series, entitled FRANK MERRIWELL'S CHUMS. But for the present all went well, and so we bid them adieu.

THE END

251

No. 2 of the MERRIWELL SERIES, entitled FRANK MER-
RIWELL'S CHUMS, is a story that will appeal to all who enjoy
having fun while keeping in mind the right thing to do at all
times. It is adventurous and fast-moving, and makes interesting
reading for all ages.